The man in creamy skin **sparked an** temptation and seduction in every graceful movement of those long limbs. Dr Finn McEwan saw guts mingled with a vulnerability that could cut a man off at the knees.

The doctor in him wondered whether Dr Juliet Adams had enough body fat to make the strenuous assault on the world's highest mountain. He knew that about fifteen per cent of body weight was lost after three months at high altitude. He had a better than fair experience of women's bodies and he was willing to bet money that Dr Adams couldn't afford to lose fifteen per cent.

Would she make it to the top of Everest?

With a soft curse, Finn reminded himself that her fitness wasn't his problem.

The fact that she was trekking to one of the most inhospitable places on earth wasn't his problem.

So why did he have a powerful urge to bundle her straight back on that terrifying flight and deliver her safely back to Kathmandu?

24:7

The cutting edge of
Mills & Boon® Medical Romance™

The emotion is deep
The drama is real
The intensity is fierce

24:7

Feel the heat—
every hour…every minute…every heartbeat

HIGH-ALTITUDE DOCTOR

BY
SARAH MORGAN

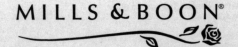

To Julian, for being perfect in every way
and for making me so happy. Love always

First published in Great Britain 2006
Harlequin Mills & Boon Limited,
Eton House, 18-24 Paradise Road, Richmond, Surrey TW9 1SR

© Sarah Morgan 2006

ISBN 0 263 84718 7

Set in Times Roman 10½ on 13 pt.
03-0306-43437

Printed and bound in Spain
by Litografia Rosés, S.A., Barcelona

CHAPTER ONE

Kathmandu, Nepal, 1300 metres above sea level

SHE was going to die.

The flight from Kathmandu to the tiny village of Lukla in the foothills of the Himalayas took only forty minutes and it was the longest, most terrifying forty minutes of her life. If there'd been any other practical way of travelling across this part of Nepal, she would have taken it.

Juliet closed her eyes tightly and tried to focus on something, *anything*, other than the clouds, the mountains hidden behind them and the ground that taunted her as it flashed beneath the aircraft.

'Hey, doc…' The bearded man in the next seat leaned towards her. 'You're looking green. You OK?'

'I will be when we land.'

'That bad, huh?' He laughed in surprise. 'And I was told you were gutsy.'

Juliet kept her eyes closed. 'My guts are back in Kathmandu. If you want to fly back and get them, Neil, that's up to you, but I'm only taking this flight once.'

The twin-engined Cessna only had sixteen seats and at that precise moment Juliet sincerely wished that there hadn't been room for her. At Kathmandu Airport hordes of people had jostled for a place on the flight but the exchange of rupees had been sufficient to ensure that all the climbers and trekkers had gained seats. Including her.

She wished she'd left a month earlier and walked.

She heard Neil give a sympathetic chuckle. 'We'll be landing soon.'

'And that's supposed to make me feel better?' Juliet opened one eye and shot him a baleful look. 'We both know what the runway is like at Lukla.'

She liked Neil Kennedy a lot. They'd climbed together in the Alps and the Himalayas and he had proved himself to be a skilful and reliable team member. He was calm, level-headed and able to smooth over the trickiest situations—a general, all-round good guy.

'They've actually built a runway?' Neil pretended to look surprised. 'That's the best news I've had all day.'

Maybe not such a good guy.

'Very funny, I'm sure.'

'Well, runway is a generous description for a bit of dirt with a cliff at the end.'

'Thanks for reminding me what it's like.'

'You were here last year. You know exactly what it's like.'

'Which is why I prefer to close my eyes.' She did so, but carried on talking. 'Are the trekkers doing OK? Anyone lost their breakfast yet?'

Four trekkers had opted to join them on the trek up to Everest base camp and Juliet knew that none of them had had any experience of high altitude before.

Neil swivelled in his seat. 'The two guys are trying to look tough and macho, one of the girls looks white and the other one is gawking out of the window at the view. She obviously doesn't know about the runway. Ten more minutes to landing and then she'll be as green as you. But so far their insides seem to still be inside.'

'Good.' She didn't want to have to think about delivering medical care to anyone at the moment. She was too busy looking after herself. 'I haven't even had a chance to get to know them yet. Do they look as though they'll make it all the way?'

'To Everest Base Camp?' Neil settled back in his seat again and gave a shrug. 'Who knows? Altitude is a great leveller, as you're always telling me. They've got all the gear and they're enthusiastic enough. And they've certainly paid enough for the privilege of trekking with Dr Juliet Adams, expert in high-altitude medicine. They think you walk on water. If anything goes wrong, they're expecting you to fix it with one wave of your magic stethoscope.'

Despite the teasing note in his voice, Juliet didn't open her eyes. At the moment she didn't feel like an expert in anything and the only thing she wanted to fix was her churning stomach. 'Well, I just hope they're impressed so far.'

'They're probably wondering how a woman who

can't open her eyes in a plane managed to climb half-way up Everest last year.'

Juliet felt a flicker of regret. 'Not the top, Neil. I had to turn back at Camp III.' Driven back by bad weather and another climber with a severe case of pulmonary oedema who had needed to be escorted down to Base Camp. The frustration and disappointment still festered inside her. *Would she have made it to the top?* 'I'm fine as long as my feet are on the ground. That's natural. It's flying that's unnatural.'

'There's nothing natural about climbing Everest,' Neil said dryly, leaning across her to stare out of the window. 'And I still don't understand what a nice girl like you is doing in a place like this. You should be at home, looking after a man and raising babies.'

'Are you proposing?'

Neil lifted her hand to his lips and gave a boyish grin. 'Believe me, if I thought I had a chance I would have proposed years ago, sweetheart. But my daughter, who is about your age, would undoubtedly die of embarrassment and my wife wouldn't be too pleased either.'

Juliet leaned across and kissed him on the cheek. 'Given that you're away from home, climbing mountains, for at least half the year, there's no way I'd marry you, but there's no one I'd rather have as part of a summit team. And this year we're going all the way to the top.'

Everest.

The highest mountain in the world.

Her goal.

'Why?' Neil let go of her hand and shot her a curious look. 'Why would a slip of a girl like you need to climb Everest?'

Something dark and terrifying stirred deep inside her, something Juliet preferred to keep locked away. She had her own reasons for being on Everest. And they were personal.

'You sound like one of those journalists.' She kept her tone light and Neil settled himself more comfortably in his seat.

'So what do you tell the journalists when they ask you that question?'

Juliet shrugged. 'Depends on my mood. If it's bad then something like, "Mind your own business." Sometimes I tell them it's because it raises my credibility when I'm lecturing a thousand doctors on high-altitude medicine.' She tilted her head to one side and gave a wry smile. 'It's hard to grab the attention of an audience if you've never been near a mountain. Sometimes I just tell them I like pushing myself to the limit.'

'And what a limit. Do you know how many people have died attempting to climb Everest?'

Her insides tensed and knotted.

Oh, yes, she knew.

'Nine per cent don't come back,' she said flatly, 'and I don't know why you're giving me this lecture, given that you're planning to climb it, too. At least I'm single.'

And she intended to stay that way.

'Is that why you never get involved with anyone? You never talk about your love life.' He turned his head and gave her a curious look. 'Do you stay single because you have a life-threatening career? Even the promise of a floaty white dress and a bunch of presents you don't need aren't enough to tempt you to marriage?'

'Now you *definitely* sound like a journalist,' Juliet said lightly, rummaging in her bag for some sweets to suck, 'and the answer is mind your own business.'

'Well, whatever the reason, I'm glad you're our team doctor. It means you can mop my fevered brow when I'm struck down by altitude. Who knows?' He gave her a saucy wink. 'I might even get mouth to mouth.'

'You should be so lucky. And, anyway, I might be the one who's struck down. Doctors don't have immunity to the effects of altitude, as you well know.' Juliet risked a glance out of the window and immediately felt her stomach lurch. 'We're coming in to land. Let's hope we live to climb a mountain instead of slamming straight into one.'

She didn't even want to think about the angle of the runway.

'There are some strong teams attempting the southeast face this year,' Neil told her, ticking them off on his fingers as he listed a few. 'There's a small Spanish team, the New Zealand team are exceptional and the Americans are filming an ascent.'

Juliet caught a glimpse of the runway ahead of her and the mountain ahead of that. She tightened her fingers into a ball and tried not to notice the abandoned wreckage of a plane on one side of the field. 'If you're trying to distract me, I have to tell you that it isn't working. You need to try harder.' She closed her eyes again and concentrated on her dream.

Everest.

Soon it would begin. The thirty-five-mile trek towards Base Camp, which would then be her home for the coming weeks.

Theoretically it was possible for an extremely fit, acclimatised person to make the distance to the foot of Everest in a few days but, as expedition doctor, Juliet had insisted that they take over a week to cover the same distance. Altitude sickness had been her area of study for several years and she understood the importance of allowing the body time to adjust to the decrease in oxygen. She was responsible for the health of the trekkers who were going with them as far as Base Camp, as well as the expedition members. And she was also responsible for her own health.

And she knew that her own health was important.

Without her, the team would have no medical back-up in a remote and potentially lethal environment.

And if she didn't stay healthy, she wouldn't be climbing the mountain.

And this year she was aiming for the summit.

She was going all the way.

Lukla, in the foothills of the Himalayas, 2850 metres above sea level

The village was tiny, little more than a cluster of huts around an airstrip, and as the plane juddered to an uneasy halt, hordes of Nepalese villagers hurried forward to unload the plane.

With her baseball cap tugged down over her eyes and her hands shoved in the pockets of her combat trousers, Juliet watched as they shifted crates and bags, checking that her medical supplies had survived the flight. Her green eyes were sharp, observant, missing nothing. Crates of vegetables, live chickens, long rolls of carpet and other cargo were mixed up with her own supplies and she watched closely as they were sorted into piles. She'd spent months calculating what she'd need to support an expedition to the world's highest mountain and she didn't want to lose any of it at this stage.

The sun blazed overhead as Neil gathered together the trekkers who had been on the flight from Kathmandu and would be joining them as far as Everest Base Camp. The rest of the climbers in their party had made the same journey a few days earlier.

Only when she was satisfied that all her packages had made it in one piece did Juliet turn away. She felt grubby and hot and in desperate need of a shower.

And that was when she spotted him.

He stood slightly apart from the other climbers and trekkers, a battered hat pulled down over his eyes, a disturbingly intent expression in his dark eyes as he watched her.

And Juliet watched him back.

What woman wouldn't have?

She saw unreasonably broad shoulders and a strong, athletic physique. She saw a man who was both arrogant and confident, a man who would lead while others followed. She saw a man who was tough and uncompromising and totally comfortable in these harsh surroundings. And she saw strong masculine features designed to make a woman dream and want.

But most of all she saw danger. The sort of danger she avoided at all costs.

For a moment Juliet struggled with her breathing. Then she told herself firmly that it was nothing to do with the fact that she was on the receiving end of that intense dark gaze, and everything to do with the sudden increase in altitude. She'd just gained six thousand feet in elevation. It was hardly surprising she was breathless.

Neil followed her gaze. 'That's Finn McEwan. Bit of a legend. He's climbed almost all the big ones, but Everest has always eluded him. Mostly because the guy is always playing the hero. Two years ago he risked his neck bringing an injured climber down from the South Col, the year before that he rescued a bunch of climbers who'd been caught in an avalanche. I hope he makes it this year. Handsome devil, isn't he? Can't believe you don't know him.'

For a moment Juliet didn't respond. She was held, locked in visual communication with the man on the opposite side of the runway. 'I've read his research,' her voice was croaky. 'I've seen him interviewed and I—'

'That's not the same,' Neil interrupted her with a wave of his hand. 'It's time you met each other in the flesh, so to speak. Come on.' He grabbed Juliet's arm. 'I'll introduce you. He's the male equivalent of you. Both doctors, both climbers, both driven and competitive. And both single.' His tone was dry. 'It's a match made in heaven.'

Panic fluttered inside her but before she could reply Neil propelled her across the airstrip and the next moment she was standing in front of the man.

'Finn.' Neil greeted the man with a handshake and a warm slap on the shoulder that suggested familiarity. Then he turned back to her. 'This dizzy-looking blonde is Dr Juliet Adams. Don't be fooled by the fact she looks like a teenager. Her qualifications are impressive. Frankly, I can't believe the two of you haven't met before now, given that you climb the same mountains, are on the same lecture circuit and the fact that you're never one to let a pretty girl pass you by, but there you are. This is your lucky moment.'

Juliet tensed, stiff with embarrassment at the introduction, but the expression on Finn McEwan's hard, handsome face didn't flicker and his gaze lingered thoughtfully on her flushed cheeks.

'Dr Adams.' He extended a hand and she had no choice but to take it. Strong fingers closed around her palm and the contact made her pulse race even faster.

In contrast he was totally relaxed, his voice deep and steady. 'I read your last paper on the effects of altitude on asthma. Your conclusions were interesting. Are you carrying out any research at the moment? What's your purpose on Everest this year?'

Juliet hesitated. 'To climb it.'

She saw something dark flicker in the depths of those dark eyes. They continued to hold hers. Continued to probe.

'You should stick to research.' His tone was low and measured. 'Or being Base Camp doctor. You shouldn't be up on her slopes.'

She lifted her chin, needled by his unwarranted advice. 'Why is that, Dr McEwan?'

There was a long silence while he watched her. 'I think you know why.'

A sudden tension snapped the air tight and for a moment his eyes held hers in silent communication.

Her stomach tumbled and her pulse raced and she cursed herself silently for feeling something she really didn't want to feel. 'I wish I had the time to argue the merits of being a woman on Everest, Dr McEwan, but I've got places I need to be.' Her tone was cool and formal and lacking in any reaction other than politeness. 'And now we need to get going because we've got some walking to do before we settle down for the night.' She jerked her hand away and turned to Neil. 'We're sleeping lower down the valley. It will be easier to breathe.'

Neil gave a slight frown. 'I know our itinerary, but I thought you—'

'We should really get going.' Aware that she was repeating herself, Juliet shifted the pack on her back and gave Finn McEwan a quick nod. 'See you at Base Camp, I expect.'

The sudden narrowing of his eyes was his only reaction to her almost curt dismissal.

'Oh, we'll see each other long before that.' His voice was a deep, lazy drawl that hinted things that she really didn't want to think about. 'We're following the same trail as you at the same pace, Dr Adams. There's a strong chance we'll get the chance to enjoy a yak burger together.'

Her gaze maintained a glacial cool. 'I don't think so. It was nice meeting you, Dr McEwan.' And with that she walked over to the trekkers, careful not to look back in case those watchful blue eyes were still trained in her direction.

'Well!' Neil joined her, not even bothering to hide his astonishment. 'What was all that about?'

Juliet bent down to adjust her boots. 'Clearly your Dr McEwan has a problem with women climbing Everest.'

Neil frowned. 'I don't think so. I mean, he's been on loads of expeditions with women. The man loves women—'

Juliet stood up. 'Must just be blondes he has a thing against, then.'

Neil shook his head. 'I don't get it. You're the most sociable person I know and normally if you meet another doctor I can't stop you talking. Finn is the best there is but you behaved as though he were carrying the plague, not here to treat it.'

Juliet didn't answer. Instead, she took her water bottle out of her pack and drank deeply. She knew the importance of keeping herself hydrated at altitude. And the activity gave her time to settle her thoughts. 'Perhaps I'm just not in the mood to argue about a woman's right to climb mountains.' She took another drink, aware that Neil was staring at her.

'But you love arguing. It's what you do best. You're sassy and sparky and you love it when people challenge you just so that you can prove them wrong.'

Juliet lowered the bottle, her peaked cap hiding the angry flash of her eyes. 'Perhaps I don't feel the need to prove myself today. We've got a schedule to keep, Neil. Let's do it.'

He stared at her. 'And that's it? You just met the heartthrob of the mountains and all you can think about are schedules?' Neil scratched his head, his expression amazed. 'You're the first woman I've ever met who hasn't gone dizzy at the sight of him. Women usually can't leave the guy alone. He's Mr Super-Cool. Real hero material.'

'Surely you mean Dr Super-Cool.' Juliet stuffed the water bottle back in her pack. 'And I don't need a hero. Let's just say that Dr Finn McEwan isn't my type.'

'But you don't know him.'

She thought of those wicked dark eyes and that lazy look that could seduce a woman at a glance. She thought of the cool self-confidence and machismo that

was part of the man. 'I know all I need to know. That
sort of guy you can read at a glance.' She checked her
boots were comfortable, swung her pack onto her pack
and jammed her cap further down over her eyes. It was
a ritual she followed before she walked. Boots, pack,
cap.

'Oh, right.' Neil gave a disbelieving laugh. 'You
don't go for strong, handsome guys who are clever
and bold as brass?'

'That's about the size of it.' Juliet shifted the pack
slightly and made a mental note to remove something
that evening. It was too heavy. She was carrying too
much gear.

'If I live to be a hundred, I will never understand
women.' Neil shook his head. 'That guy scores with
every female he meets. He fights them off.'

'Sounds exhausting. I'm sure he'll be relieved to
know that I'm one less woman he'll have to keep at a
distance.' She strolled towards the trekkers who were
hovering, determined not to let her mind linger on Finn
McEwan for even a second. He didn't think she should
be on Everest. But she wasn't interested in his opinion, she reminded herself. His opinion didn't matter to
her. 'I just want to watch them load my medical equipment and then we'll start the walk to the village. The
sun is hot at the moment but once it dips behind those
clouds the temperature will drop sharply so make sure
you have an extra layer handy.'

Sally, one of the trekkers, walked over to her. 'That
flight was amazing. I couldn't believe the angle of the

runway.' She was obviously eager to ask questions. 'Is it true that it's possible to walk to Everest Base Camp in three days from here?'

Juliet ignored Neil's pained expression. The trekkers had paid to be guided by a doctor with experience in high-altitude medicine. They had a right to ask questions and she was more than happy to answer them. This was her job. It was what she knew. *And she was happy to be distracted from thoughts of Finn McEwan.* 'If you want to risk cutting your holiday short, yes. But from this point on you're going to feel the effects of high altitude. If you don't give yourself time to acclimatise, you'll suffer. You need to give your body time to adjust to having less oxygen. Climb too high, too fast and your trip will be over. And not just the trip. Over supper tonight I'm going to give a talk on altitude sickness so that you all know the basics.' A small crowd of Sherpas converged on the luggage and Juliet's face brightened as one of them approached her, a broad smile on his face. 'Pemba Sherpa! Our Base Camp leader. *Namaste.*'

Using her rusty and very limited Nepali, she greeted the Sherpa whom she'd met on previous expeditions and who would be responsible for running the camp that they established at the base of the mountain. She switched to English to discuss the transportation of her medical equipment and watched as a string of yaks were led onto the landing field.

Yaks, a type of hardy cattle, were used to transport packs and equipment up to Base Camp and Juliet watched in trepidation as the Sherpas placed blankets and wooden frames on the animals' backs and then started tying on her crates. Would they be too heavy? She'd barely been able to lift half of them but the animal didn't flinch and she relaxed slightly when she saw that the Sherpas were loading still more on top. Clearly they didn't consider her supplies to be excessively heavy.

Which was a relief, because she'd carefully run through all the possible medical scenarios that she was likely to encounter on the barren, frozen flanks of Everest and she'd packed accordingly. She didn't want to leave any of the equipment behind.

Juliet stood and watched, slim as a blade, her blonde hair falling in a plait between her narrow shoulder-blades, her mind totally focused on the job in hand. Only when she was satisfied that it was all safely loaded did she turn her attention back to the trekkers.

'This isn't a particularly nice place to linger and I want us to sleep at a lower altitude tonight to make breathing easier, so we've got a short walk ahead of us down to the hamlet where we'll be staying.' She'd planned the route carefully with Billy, their expedition leader, who would be meeting up with them at Base Camp.

The trail was hard-packed dirt and easy to follow and Juliet soon settled into her stride, enjoying the rhythm and the stimulation of physical exercise, taking the time to review the people walking with her. In fact, she was careful to think about everything except Dr Finn McEwan.

A clear vision of him came into her mind and she dismissed it instantly.

Base Camp was going to be busy, she assured herself. Once the season started there could be as many as six hundred people camped on the glacier. It was like a small town and each expedition had their own goals and objectives. Dr Finn McEwan would have plenty to occupy him.

He wouldn't have time to concern himself with her or her reasons for being on Everest. And she certainly wouldn't have time to concern herself with him.

Sally closed in behind her, still eager to talk. 'I can't believe I'm really here. In the Himalayas. It's been my dream for so long.'

Grateful for the distraction, Juliet encouraged her to chat and learned that she and the other trekkers were all medical students.

They were an enthusiastic and lively bunch and Juliet hoped that they weren't underestimating the effects that altitude would have as they climbed further down the valley. Many people who had never been exposed to the effects of high altitude were taken by surprise.

Just as she'd predicted, as soon as the sun vanished behind the clouds, the temperature dropped dramatically. Juliet stopped to pull a jumper out of her pack. 'The air doesn't hold much heat up here,' she told Sally. 'Once the sun goes, it's freezing.'

Sally also added another layer and Juliet noticed that she was slightly out of breath.

Lack of fitness, excitement or the sudden increase in altitude? Juliet wondered at the cause and made a mental note to keep an eye on Sally.

They continued down the trail to the river, crossed a wood and cable suspension bridge and arrived in the tiny hamlet that would be their home for the night.

A group of climbers was sitting outside a lodge with their feet up, drinking Coke, and Juliet exchanged a few words of greeting and then took Sally up a set of steps to a top-floor room that was full of wooden bunks.

'We'll bag a space now,' she told Sally, 'ready for when our duffel bags arrive. Make sure you keep your day pack as light as you can. Only carry the things you really need. Everything else—spare film, sleeping bags—put in your duffel.'

All items not needed during the day and which were to be carried by the Sherpas were packed into duffel bags, leaving the climbers and trekkers to carry the bare minimum as they negotiated the trail through the foothills.

Sally glanced around her, her gaze sharp and interested. 'How do they build these things in the middle of nowhere?'

'Hard work.' Juliet rummaged in her pack for another jumper. 'You see Sherpas and yaks transporting impossible loads up and down the valley. Teahouses and lodges are springing up all over the trail now to accommodate trekkers and climbers, some of them more sanitary than others, to be honest. When we get higher up we'll be moving into tents. Come on—let's join the others and get something to eat. Then I'm going to brief you all so that you're prepared for what's ahead.'

CHAPTER TWO

THEY ate sardines and French fries and afterwards, she and Neil gathered the trekkers together in the small, smoky room of the teahouse that served as a dining area when it was too cold to sit outside. In one corner a fire burned and at a table in the corner sat two climbers. One of them was Finn McEwan.

The moment Juliet entered the room their eyes met and held. Then she forced herself to give a nod of acknowledgement and turned her attention to her own party. She would have preferred that he wasn't sitting in the corner while she talked, but there was nothing she could do about it. So she set about ignoring him.

'Tomorrow we've got a five-hour, three-thousand-metre climb to the village of Namche Bazaar.' She spread out the map so that she could show them the route. 'You could call it the last outpost of civilisation. It may not seem far but it's really important that you walk slowly. At this altitude you can get tired very quickly and if you exhaust yourselves early on, you won't be finishing the trek. Remember the story of the hare and the tortoise? Well, up here, it's the tortoise that wins every time.'

One of the men settled back in his chair, his arms hooked behind his head, gym-developed muscles bunched. 'We're all pretty fit and well prepared.' His gaze was slightly mocking, as if it should have been obvious from a glance that he was more than up to the job. 'I can't see any of us having a problem.'

Cocky.

Juliet studied him for a moment, looked at the muscles and the man and wondered whether to cut him down to size now or let him fall down by himself later. His name was Simon and she'd met his sort before on treks. Macho. Determined to stride out and prove himself, not understanding the effects of altitude on human physiology. By the next day he'd probably be gasping for breath by the side of the trail, unwilling to admit that he was in trouble.

In the interests of team harmony, she decided to watch and wait. But she delivered a polite warning. After all, that was her job and if she didn't watch him, she'd be the one clearing up the mess.

'The only thing that can prepare you for altitude is altitude itself.' She spoke the words quietly, directly to him, hoping that he'd take heed. Then she addressed the group as a whole. 'As we get higher up we'll be sleeping two to a tent, and as soon as you arrive in the camp the Sherpas will serve tea. Make sure you drink it. It's important to drink plenty of liquid at high altitudes and in hot weather to prevent dehydration. Due to the polluted water supplies it is necessary to boil all water, so hot tea is the best available drink. Having said that…' Juliet gave a wry smile '…heartburn is a common complaint around here and it's largely due to the tannin in the black tea. It's abrasive and irritating to the stomach. If you find you have problems, you might want to switch to herbal.'

The two guys exchanged appalled looks that clearly stated their opinion of herbal tea.

Juliet chose to ignore them, knowing that once their stomachs started protesting they'd switch soon enough. Instead, she ran a finger over the map, showing them the route. 'The first half of tomorrow's trail follows the river and crosses it a few times. Then we gain some height and that's when you'll start to feel the effects of altitude. I've said it before but I'm going to say it again because it's important.' She lifted her head and looked directly at Simon, determined to get the message across. 'You need to keep your pace slow and steady.'

He gave a suggestive smile. 'I can do slow and steady when the occasion demands it. Any time you want a demonstration, Doc, you only have to ask.'

'You're totally disgusting, Si.' Sally gave him a friendly thump on the shoulder and leaned forward to look at the map more closely, her expression interested. 'Can you really develop altitude sickness at that elevation? I thought you'd need to be higher up to feel the effects.'

Juliet chose to ignore Simon's comment but the look in his eyes was making her increasingly uneasy about the forthcoming trip. 'Certain normal physiological changes occur in every person who goes to altitude. At night you wake more frequently and you might notice a difference in your breathing pattern. During the day you'll find that you become short of breath on exertion and you need to pass urine more often.'

'All the more reason to cut down on that herbal tea,' Simon drawled, and Juliet gritted her teeth and reflected on the fact that before the trip was over she might well have stabbed the guy with the business end of her ice axe.

She didn't like his arrogance and she didn't like the way he was looking at her.

Something made her glance across at Finn and she was surprised to find him staring at Simon, his gaze cold and hard.

Juliet bit her lip, wondering exactly what had angered him. Perhaps she wasn't the only person to find the guy objectionable.

Sally sipped her drink, apparently oblivious to the undercurrents of tension around the table. Or maybe she was just used to Simon. 'And that's all OK? All those changes are normal?'

'As long as the shortness of breath resolves rapidly once you take some rest. The increase in breathing is an essential part of adapting to the altitude. You have to work harder to obtain oxygen and you do it by breathing more deeply and more quickly.'

'Because there is less oxygen in the air?'

'Precisely.'

The other male trekker, Gary, was enjoying a drink of chang, the local brew, and Juliet gave him a pointed look. 'That can be a pretty alcoholic drink and by tomorrow you might be regretting that decision. It's a good idea to avoid alcohol and certain drugs, anything that might decrease breathing—that's if you want to finish the trek. Remember, you need those extra breaths to give your body the oxygen it needs to function. And even when you're breathing faster you still won't gain normal blood levels of oxygen.'

Simon stared at the glass. 'No alcohol and plenty of herbal tea. Who the hell talked me into this trip?'

Sally frowned at him. 'For goodness sake, shut up, Si.'

Silently thanking Sally for the timely intervention, Juliet continued with her talk, aware that Neil had joined Finn and was watching and listening from the edge of the room.

An oldtimer at altitude, Neil had seen it all before. And heard it all before.

Juliet carried on talking, made the points she wanted to make, answered the girls' many questions and then called a halt to the evening.

She needed some space and time by herself.

And she needed to get away from Simon.

Leaving the group of trekkers to enjoy themselves, she dragged on her jacket and left the teahouse, braving the freezing air outside.

Juliet stood for a moment with her eyes closed, feeling the sting of the cold bite her cheeks and listening to the rush of the river just below the lodge. She breathed in the smell of smoke and outdoors and instantly felt more relaxed. Apart from the muffled laughter that came from within the lodge, the night was silent and she huddled deeper inside her jacket and opened her eyes, letting her vision adjust to the semi-darkness.

She walked a short distance, sat down on a boulder and hugged her knees, enjoying the night sounds.

'That trekker of yours is going to give you a problem. You need to watch him.'

The deep, masculine voice came from right next to her and she gave a soft gasp, wondering how she could have not noticed the powerful figure leaning against the tree.

It was Finn McEwan.

He was obviously escaping the crowds, too.

She stared into his strong, handsome face and felt her heart beat faster. Frustration at her own unexpected reaction to him made her more irritable than usual. 'Thanks for your concern but I don't need your advice on how to handle arrogant men,' she said, resisting the temptation to scramble to her feet and take refuge inside the lodge. She'd wanted some air and she was going to stay put. No one was going to drive her away. 'Simon will be fine once he recognises the effects of altitude.'

There was a long pause. 'I wasn't referring to his fitness levels, although you and I both know those muscles aren't going to help him much up here.' Finn's tone was even. 'I was referring to the way he was looking at you. And if you didn't notice then you're not the woman I think you are. A woman who thinks she's smart enough to get herself up Everest should be smart enough to sense a problem when it's staring her in the face, and that guy is trouble.'

Juliet felt a flicker of unease. She wanted to argue with him but she couldn't because she knew he was right. Simon was trouble. 'I can handle it,' she said calmly, stuffing her hands deep in her pockets to keep them warm. 'I was brought up dealing with trouble. You don't need to worry about me.'

She certainly didn't want him worrying about her.

She wished he'd go inside and leave her to enjoy the cold night alone but he didn't shift, his broad shoulders planted against the tree, his eyes watchful. She was aware of the hard planes of his handsome face, the steady rhythm of his breathing as his breath clouded the freezing air. Together they shared the darkness and it felt as though they were the only two people in this corner of the world.

The forced intimacy unsettled her, especially as he seemed reluctant to drop the subject.

'Take my advice,' he drawled softly. 'Keep Neil close by at all times.'

She gave a little shiver and her own sense of unease escalated. 'I don't need a bodyguard to keep an over-persistent man at a distance. You don't need to worry about me.'

There was a long silence while he watched her and

then he stirred, obviously intending to respond. 'Dr Adams—'

'No!' Juliet lifted a hand and interrupted him hastily, before he could say what she suspected he was going to say. 'I know that some men are very protective towards women but I don't need your protection—and I don't want it. I'm fine on my own. I'm used to being on my own.'

'Calm down.' Finn's tone was level. Neutral. 'I'm just looking out for a colleague.'

Juliet stared at him for a long moment and felt something stir inside her. *Felt something she definitely didn't want to feel.* 'I'm not in trouble, Dr McEwan, and I'm not your colleague. We're two strangers who just happen to have our sights set on the same mountain. That doesn't make us colleagues.'

It was a warning.

Don't come any closer.

His gaze didn't shift from her face. 'Up on that mountain, we're all part of the same team, you know that as well as I do. The fortunes of one person are inextricably linked with all the others,' he drawled softly, strolling across to her and pausing only inches away from where she was seated. 'Which brings me to my next question. What are you doing here, Dr Adams? What the hell are you doing here?'

Her heart beat faster. 'Why shouldn't I be here?' Juliet rose to her feet, flustered and boiling with frustration, and then wished she'd remained seated because standing merely brought her closer to Finn

McEwan and closer to Finn McEwan was one place she really, *really* didn't want to be.

He stood within touching distance, hard and tough, a man with a strength, maturity and presence that set him apart from other men. It crossed her mind that he made Simon look like an adolescent—over-eager to score with women and then brag of his successes. Still very much a boy despite the outward appearance of manhood.

In contrast, there was nothing of the boy in Finn McEwan. He was all man.

She felt a throb of awareness deep inside her—something sexual that she'd long denied.

'I'm doing exactly what you're doing, Dr McEwan.' In an attempt to halt the slow, insidious curl low in her pelvis, Juliet took several steps backwards, increasing the distance between them. 'Combining my interest in high-altitude medicine with my love of climbing.'

Finn didn't comment on her retreat but she knew his eyes had noticed the movement. She saw the sudden narrowing and the silent question in those dark depths.

'Climbing Everest is hardly an everyday sort of hobby,' he said mildly, and she tilted her chin, aiming for angry. Angry was so much safer than sexually aware.

'Do you feel threatened by strong women, Finn?' Her eyes flashed him a challenge. 'Are you more comfortable with stereotypes? Do you expect a woman to stay at home and knit and bake cakes while waiting for her man to return from a day's hunting?'

There was a moment's silence while he scanned her face, his expression thoughtful. 'I think a person should be whatever they want to be,' he said finally, 'and should travel in whatever direction they wish to travel in life, irrespective of sex or age.'

Her eyes clashed with his and held for a long, breathless moment. Her heart stumbled in her chest. 'So why don't you think a woman like me should be on the mountain?'

'I suppose I'm just wondering whether you're doing what you want to do or whether something else entirely is driving you.' He looked at her with that lazy, masculine scrutiny that she found so unsettling. 'What exactly are you doing here, Dr Adams?'

This wasn't a conversation that she wanted to have. 'I don't know what you mean.'

'No?' His gaze didn't shift from hers. 'Mountains are harsh and unforgiving. They make man feel strong and invincible and then reveal him as puny. They force you to take risks and then make you pay, possibly the ultimate price. Is that what you want? Are those the risks you truly want to take?'

Her heart beat a little faster. 'I don't take risks, Dr McEwan.'

His mouth curved into a faint smile. 'Just being here is a risk, and you know that as well as I do. You could get seriously hurt, or worse.'

'Maybe we have a different definition of risk. I happen to call this living.' As if to illustrate her point, she breathed in deeply and glanced around her, her green

eyes shining in the semi-darkness. 'And as for hurt…'
She gave a tiny shrug. 'It doesn't matter where you go
or what you do in life, you can't avoid being hurt. I can
play it safe and still manage to get hurt. I can be hit by
a bus, stabbed by a patient and I can get my heart broken by a man.'

There was the briefest of pauses and when Finn
spoke his voice sounded strangely harsh in the cold
night air. 'And is that what happened to you, Dr
Adams? Did you get your heart broken by a man?'

Tension throbbed between them and for a moment
Juliet couldn't find the breath to speak. She pushed the
memories back into the past and reminded herself that
climbing a mountain was all about moving forward in
slow steps. And life was like a mountain. 'It was just
a phrase. Hearts don't break, Dr McEwan.' She tilted
her head, ignoring the fact that her pulse was dancing
a jig. It was the altitude, she told herself. Just the altitude. 'Arteries get clogged, valves degenerate and muscles weaken and die, but hearts don't break. You're a
doctor. You should know that.'

He inhaled sharply. 'I know that there's a great deal
about the human body we don't understand.'

'And never will. A bit like life.' She gave a little shiver
and wrapped her arms around her waist. 'It's getting
cold. I'm going back inside. Goodnight, Dr McEwan.'

Finn's hesitation was barely perceptible. 'Goodnight,
Dr Adams. Sleep well.'

She knew she wouldn't and she suspected he knew
that, too.

As she walked away, she thought she heard him mutter, 'And if there's a lock on your door, use it.' But she decided that she must have imagined it.

Finn stood still in the dark and the cold and watched Juliet go. He wanted to call her back, wanted to make her stay and talk long into the night until he'd got right inside her head, but instead he kept silent and watched the door swing closed behind her, his last glimpse of her focused on the blonde plait that hung down her back.

The man in him saw soft curves, creamy skin and green eyes that sparked and teased. He saw temptation and seduction in every graceful movement of those long limbs. He saw guts mingled with a vulnerability that could cut a man off at the knees.

The doctor in him wondered whether she had enough body fat to make the strenuous assault on the world's highest mountain. He knew that about fifteen per cent of body weight was lost after three months at high altitude. He had a better than fair experience of women's bodies and he was willing to bet money that Dr Adams couldn't afford to lose fifteen per cent.

Would she make it to the top of Everest?

With a soft curse he reminded himself that her fitness wasn't his problem.

The fact that she was trekking to one of the most inhospitable places on earth wasn't his problem.

Finn was used to climbing with strong women and he would never have dreamed of offering assistance unless it was requested. So why was she different? Why did he suddenly have a need to switch teams and anchor himself firmly to her side for the duration of the expedition?

Why did he have a powerful urge to bundle her straight back on that terrifying flight and deliver her safely back to Kathmandu?

Finn let out a vicious curse and reminded himself that feeling over-protective was his problem. She'd made it clear enough that she wouldn't welcome his interference or his protection.

And he had no right to offer it.

'Climb, Jules, Climb!'

Juliet was eight years old and clinging to a rockface in frozen terror while her big brother grinned down at her from above. Daniel Adams. Daredevil and wild boy. To her he was a god. Fourteen years old and totally fearless, whereas she could hardly breathe for fear. It gripped her in its jaws like a wild beast, preventing movement, and now she was stuck, clinging to the exposed rockface, paralysed by the enormity of the risk she was taking. 'I'm going to fall!'

Her fingers tightened in the tiny crack and her toes felt numb.

She was going to let go.

'You're not going to fall and even if you do, I'll catch you because we're roped together.' Her brother's voice was impatient. 'Look up, not down. Concentrate. Feel the rock. Go for it, Jules, you can do it! You're my sister!'

A moment of delicious pride mingled with the panic.

She didn't want to go for it. She just wanted to curl up in a ball away from risk, but she'd discovered that the biggest high on earth was her older brother's approval. And she couldn't fall because to fall would be to fail and no one in her family ever failed at anything.

Everyone in her family was bold and fearless and kicked against the life-throttling ropes of convention. And she was going to be the same.

So she closed her eyes and tried to forget the drop beneath her.

She tried to forget that climbing terrified her. She tried to forget that heights made her stomach roll.

And she climbed.

Upwards, towards her brother's approving smile. Her brother always smiled. And he was still smiling when he lost his footing moments later and plunged headlong down the sheer rockface, dragging her with him into a dark, dark void of terror and death.

CHAPTER THREE

JULIET woke in a sweat, her breathing rapid and her pulse thundering, a sick feeling deep in the pit of her stomach.

Darkness still engulfed the room and she had a frantic need to turn on the light, to remove the feeling of menace that pressed down on her. But the other occupants of the room were still sleeping and she knew she couldn't make a sound. To do so would be to attract attention and she didn't want attention. She needed privacy to compose herself and drag her mind back into a comfortable place.

So instead she sat upright on her bunk and hooked her arms around her knees, trying to breathe slowly and think boring daytime thoughts. Trying to push away the lingering tentacles of the nightmare. But even in her state of full wakefulness, the images lingered, frighteningly vivid and all too real.

Why now, when she hadn't had the dream for years? *Why tonight?*

Her mouth was dry and she reached for her water bottle and drank deeply.

She knew why, of course. She knew exactly why.

The memory would fade, she reminded herself as she replaced the top on her water bottle and lay down on her bunk, knowing that she wouldn't sleep again that night.

She didn't dare, in case the dream came back again.

So she lay in the dark, listening to the rhythmic breathing of the others in the room and fighting off the demons of her past.

Despite her fears, Juliet dozed off only to wake again at six, freezing cold and with a thumping headache.

Stress or the first signs of altitude sickness?

She tugged on extra layers and carefully packed her duffel bag ready for the Sherpas to add to their load. Then she joined the others for breakfast, hoping they were in better shape than her.

They were eating omelette and fried bread and instantly she could see that both Gary and Simon looked the worse for wear, although the two girls seemed quite lively.

'How was your night?' She addressed the two men without any great confidence that they'd tell her the truth. She'd already decided that she was going to have to find a way of breaking down those macho barriers so that she could gain a real picture of their physical state.

She made a mental note to talk to each of the young men separately, hoping that without peer pressure they might be prepared to open up.

They lingered over breakfast and were just packing up to leave when one of their Sherpas came running along the path towards them.

'Dr Juliet, you need to come. Cook has accident.'

Juliet grabbed the pack that contained a basic first-aid kit and followed him without question, wondering what had happened.

Despite the availability of accommodation, the Sherpas preferred to set up their own tent and one of them had managed to cut himself badly while preparing breakfast.

He was sitting on a boulder, blood pouring from his finger, a horrified expression on his face.

'I need some water, Pemba,' Juliet instructed quickly, delving into her pack and dragging out her first-aid kit. She cleaned the wound so that she could get a better look at what was going on and decided that it wasn't going to need stitches.

'Wound very deep,' Pemba said sorrowfully, and Juliet gave him a reassuring smile.

'It's not that deep, Pemba. I'll give it a proper clean and put some steristrips on it.'

'Stitches?'

'Paper stitches,' Juliet amended, but he nodded with satisfaction and she decided it really didn't matter whether he thought they were proper stitches or not. The finger would be treated and that was what counted.

As expedition doctor she was responsible for the health of the Sherpas as well as the Western climbers and trekkers, and she took that responsibility very seriously indeed. In her opinion they were all entitled to the same care. In truth, the injury was minor, but she didn't want them to think that they were less important to her so she gave the injury more attention than she otherwise might have done.

Once the finger was securely dressed she rose to her feet and swung her pack onto her back.

'It should be fine, but if it gives you a problem, let me know.'

The injured Sherpa gazed at his neatly bandaged finger with pride and Juliet hid a smile.

He was like a child, seeking attention.

She rejoined her party at the teahouse and finally they set off, following the trail that would lead them to the next village.

Neil led and Juliet stayed at the back, intending to sweep up any stragglers and hoping for some peace and quiet to sort out her pounding headache.

She was out of luck.

'Good morning, Dr Adams.' It was Finn McEwan, looking rested and relaxed and disturbingly handsome. Dark stubble covered his jaw and he'd stripped down to a T-shirt, exposing broad shoulders and hard muscle. He looked strong and fit and more than capable of tackling the word's highest mountain.

In comparison she felt tired and weak and every step was a monumental effort.

She stood to one side to let him pass. 'I expect you want to get going,' she said politely, 'so feel free to overtake.'

His eyes rested on her face. 'You're looking pale, Dr Adams. Bad night?'

She tensed, remembering the nightmares. *And the cause of them.* 'I slept fine,' she lied. 'How about you?'

'Never better.' He looked at her thoughtfully. 'Maybe you should spend another day here if the altitude is bothering you.'

'The altitude isn't bothering me,' she said immediately, and his eyes narrowed.

'Which means that something else is. Anything you want to talk about?'

She looked him straight in the eye. 'What would I possibly want to talk about?'

He was silent for a long moment, his eyes on her face. 'Obviously nothing.'

'That's right.' She gave him a bright smile that took the last of her energy. 'Glad to see you in such good form, Dr McEwan. I'm sure nothing will hold you back today. Are you walking with your group?'

He shook his head. 'We're all traveling independently and meeting at Base Camp. So I'm more than happy to provide extra muscle for your expedition, Dr Adams.'

Her heart sank. She really, *really* didn't want him hanging around. 'We're fine,' she said stiffly, 'and we're going to take it slowly today so you might want to just do your own thing.'

Please, let him do his own thing. The last thing she needed was his company on the trek.

But if she was hoping he'd take the hint and walk on

up the trail she was doomed to disappointment because he stayed close to her, and at that moment Sally joined them.

'Dr McEwan!' Her pretty face flushed pink with delight when she saw him and she fell into step beside him. 'I've got your textbook on high-altitude medicine on my bookshelf at home and your book on climbing. I've read it and reread it. It's amazing.'

Irritated by the blatant hero-worship, Juliet gritted her teeth but Finn simply looked amused.

'Well, that's nice. Always good to meet a fan.'

'Are you planning to reach the summit this time or are you doing research?'

'Both, hopefully,' Finn said pleasantly, 'but you never really know. Mountains have a habit of making decisions for you. You climb when and if they allow it.'

It was still early and frost winked and flickered as they started up the trail by the side of a boulder-strewn river that sent turquoise water crashing down into the valley.

Finally Finn moved ahead of them and Juliet felt herself start to relax.

'The water runs off the glacier,' she told Sally as they strolled along together at a steady pace, 'so it's icy cold.'

They crossed a rickety bridge that ran over the river and Sally stared at a pile of wood neatly stacked to one side of the path. 'What's the wood for?'

Juliet shifted the pack on her back. 'When the river

floods the bridges are often washed away and have to be rebuilt. The wood is there ready for the next bridge.' She glanced at Sally's pale face and laughed. 'You signed on for adventure, remember?'

Sally pulled a face. 'Plunging into a ravine wasn't what I had in mind.'

As they walked the sun grew hotter and they all stripped off layers and tucked them safely away in their day packs.

'I've read so much about your work,' Sally chatted away, 'and I've read about Dr McEwan. I've drooled over his photo on the front of his book but he's even better-looking in real life, isn't he? He's *loaded,* did you know that? His family is seriously wealthy. That's the reason he can afford to finance all those expeditions he tackles. Last year Antarctica and this year Everest. He's rich, good-looking, with a body to die for, and he's still single. Can you believe that?'

Juliet concentrated on the trail.

Yes, she could believe that. She understood about being single. And she was trying hard not to think about Finn McEwan's body. 'The man is never in the same place for more than five minutes so I can't imagine he's in a position to have a relationship or consider marriage.'

Sally looked at her. 'So when you're not climbing, you work in an A and E department?'

'I do locums.' Juliet shifted her pack on her back. 'I prefer it that way. It means I don't get locked in. It's hard to persuade an employer to give you three months off every spring so that you can vanish to the Himalayas.'

'But surely you won't want to do that for ever? Won't you want to settle down and get married?'

Juliet kept her eyes forward. 'I'm not very good at staying in one place,' she said eventually. 'And marriage isn't for everyone.'

Something flickered inside her and she pushed it away. She'd never been interested in settling down, and she never would be.

She needed to know that she could just pack a bag and go, wherever she wanted to go, whenever she wanted to go there, without reference to another person.

She needed to know that her heart wouldn't be broken.

She walked deep in thought as the path snaked through rhododendrons and fragrant blue pine and fir. A little later they crossed the river again into the Sagarmartha National Park.

They stopped at the guard post so that Neil could deal with the special permits that they'd purchased in Kathmandu.

'Why all the security?' Simon muttered, watching while an armed guard checked all the paperwork.

'Because selling permits is big business to them,' Neil told him. 'No one gets in unless they've paid. They're also monitoring the traders. There's a large military base not far from here.'

The guards were clearly satisfied with what they

saw because the group was allowed to pass and Juliet swung her pack off her back and drank, exhorting the others to do the same.

'Don't forget the importance of keeping hydrated,' she said, and Neil grinned.

'You could say it's all uphill from here, so we'll take a break, have some lunch and then get stuck in. Brace yourselves for some amazing views.'

They ate lunch in the blazing heat and Juliet took advantage of the break to strip down to shorts and a T-shirt.

Then they continued over a huge metal bridge hanging two hundred feet above the tumbling river below and from there the trail climbed steadily upwards towards the Sherpa village of Namche Bazaar.

Neil kept the pace slow and Juliet followed in the rear, ready to check on any stragglers who might be struggling to keep up.

From here they could see Everest and Sally stopped dead and reached for her camera.

'I can't believe you're actually planning to climb to the top of that,' she breathed. 'It looks so far away.'

Juliet stared towards the mountain and wondered what it had planned for them.

What dramas would take place on her slopes this year? Would she claim more lives?

Sally stowed her camera safely in her day pack. 'There's hardly any snow on the top.'

'The summit of Everest is in the jet stream. Eighty-mile-an-hour winds make it impossible to climb for almost all of the year.' Juliet stared at the awe-inspiring triangular jut of black rock that was Everest's summit and felt something dark and terrifying curl inside her. 'But around May, the warm winds of the monsoon raise the height of the winds by a few thousand feet and then, if you're very lucky, for a short time it's climbable, providing you're high up the mountain at the time.'

'I've heard that just about any fit person could get up there,' Simon said, adjusting his shades and staring at the peak.

Juliet stilled for a moment and then turned to look at him, her expression blank. 'People who underestimate Everest tend to pay the price,' she said quietly, shifting her pack on her shoulders. 'Let's go.'

She would have liked time to be on her own with her thoughts but he fell into step beside her, obviously intent on charming her.

'So, Dr Adams…' his smile flashed '…what does your boyfriend think about this unconventional job of yours?'

He was fishing.

Accustomed to dodging personal questions from persistent journalists eager for a story, she gave a bland smile. 'My boyfriend is kept pretty busy with his martial arts and boxing,' she replied with good humour, 'so it's not a problem.'

He cast a speculative look in her direction. 'If you were mine I wouldn't let you out of my sight.'

'Then it's fortunate I'm not yours.' She changed the

subject neatly and then dropped back to join Sally, who was dropping behind. 'How are you doing?'

Sally stopped to breath. 'Fine.' She wiped her forehead with her forearm. 'But I'm not as quick as the others.'

'Up here, slow is good,' Juliet reminded her. 'It isn't a race. Don't worry. You're doing well.'

Juliet purposefully slowed her pace and walked with Sally, encouraging and distracting her as they moved leisurely up the trail.

In the end the two men and Diane, the other trekker, strode ahead with Neil, and Juliet and Sally arrived in the Sherpa village of Namche Bazaar almost two hours behind them.

'It looks like an amphitheatre,' Sally said breathlessly, gazing upwards at the village, which nestled in a bowl halfway up a mountainside.

Juliet nodded. 'It's surprisingly developed. It has bakeries, email facilities and the market on a Saturday is great.'

'Will we have time to explore?'

'Tomorrow is a rest day.' Juliet smiled at her. 'But we recommend that you trek higher and then come back down to sleep. It helps the acclimatisation process. But there'll certainly be time to look around.'

She led Sally along a series of narrow paths that led between the buildings until they reached the lodge that would be their home for the night.

The others were already gathered around a table, drinking tea—apart from Simon, who was drinking beer.

Finn McEwan had joined them. His hard jaw was dark with stubble and he looked sexier than any man had a right to look.

His eyes met Juliet's and for a long moment they just stared at each other.

Sally took the pack off her back with a sigh of relief. 'We made it in the end, folks,' she said breathlessly. 'Better late than never.'

'We'd almost given up on you,' Simon said, a mocking expression in his eyes.

Juliet dragged her gaze away from Finn, thoroughly disturbed by the sudden increase in her pulse rate. Why was he affecting her like this? 'I hope you didn't overdo it today,' she said to the other three trekkers, grasping at the opportunity for distraction. 'I want you to tell me if you have any headaches.'

Simon rolled the bottle between his fingers and grinned at the others. 'After a night on the beer, if I don't get a headache then I'm demanding a refund.'

Finn's eyes narrowed. 'You might want to moderate your alcohol consumption,' he drawled lightly, and Simon lifted the beer to his lips, a flash of irritation showing in his eyes.

'On the other hand, I might not.'

Finn didn't answer and Neil rolled his eyes and gave a shrug, a good-natured smile on his face. 'It's good advice, mate. Take it or you're going to regret it in the morning.'

Dinner was served by a girl dressed in traditional Sherpa dress. They ate, talked and then Diane and

Sally retired to bed early while the men stayed up drinking.

Stifled by the smoke in the dining room, Juliet went outside for air and was immediately followed by Simon, who had obviously been waiting for the opportunity to get her on her own.

He slung an arm around her shoulders. 'This place is great. Really great. And you're one hell of a woman, Dr Adams.'

His words were slightly slurred and Juliet moved to one side in an attempt to extricate herself from his grip, but he merely tightened his arm and pulled her against him.

'How about a little holiday romance?' he drawled, and cupped her face, bringing his mouth down on hers.

Juliet shoved hard. 'Get off!'

He released her and staggered, swaying for a moment as he attempted to keep his balance. 'If that's supposed to put me off then you'll have to try harder. I love a woman with attitude.' He reached for her again but this time a strong hand closed over his shoulder and hauled him away.

It was Finn. 'Do you have a problem?' His tone was pleasant but his eyes were hard and his expression grim and purposeful. 'Dr Adams said no.'

Simon's eyes narrowed as he tried to focus. 'And why would you care? Or have you got your eye on her, too?'

Finn's jaw tightened. 'Go upstairs and sleep it off,' he advised in an icy tone. 'And don't forget to apologise in the morning.'

Simon swayed and he studied the breadth of Finn's shoulders. Then he gave a shrug and lurched through the doorway back into the lodge, leaving Juliet alone with Finn.

Snow was falling steadily and the night air was freezing.

Finn strolled over to her side. 'You need to watch the company you keep.'

Her heart was thumping and she felt more than a little shocked by what had happened. 'I can take care of myself.' But her voice shook slightly and Finn studied her for a long moment and then glanced back towards the lodge.

'Evidently not.'

'Finn.' Juliet scraped a strand of hair behind her ear. 'Thanks for your help, but I can manage. I don't need you to look out for me.'

Those blue eyes rested on her face. 'As long as you're climbing that mountain, I'll be watching out for you.' He took a deep breath. 'Don't climb, Juliet.'

She stiffened, thrown by the sudden change of subject. 'I beg your pardon?'

'Don't do it.' His voice was deep and purposeful. 'Stay at Base Camp and act as doctor, but don't climb that mountain.'

'*You're* intending to climb it.'

'That's different.'

'Because you're a man and I'm a woman?'

He stared at her for a long moment. 'No. Not because of that.'

'What, then?'

There was a strange light in his dark eyes. 'Tell me.' His tone was pleasant, almost casual. 'Just how long are you planning to carry on this pretence that we don't know each other? For just how long are we expected to act like total strangers?'

Her heart pounded and suddenly there wasn't enough oxygen in the air. She glanced behind her to check that they were on their own. 'For the entire expedition. People are living in each other's pockets, you know that as well as I do. The last thing people need up here is emotional baggage and conflict and, anyway, it was all a long time ago. Ten years ago, Finn. We don't know each other any more.'

His gaze rested on her flushed cheeks. 'Jules.' His voice was soft. 'I know you as well as it is possible for a man to know a woman. I know every single inch of you. I know how your body works, how your mind works. And I know what scares you and what drives you. And I know what's driving you now.'

Her body heated and trembled at his blunt reference to the past and she wrapped her arms round her as if to protect herself.

She didn't want to remember the past. It was all too complicated.

Too painful.

And she didn't want to remember the way Finn had made her feel.

'It's in the past, Finn. And that's where it's staying. I don't want to discuss it. I really don't want to talk about any of it.' Their relationship was all wrapped up in a time she preferred to forget.

'Why?' He slipped his fingers under her chin and tilted her face to his. 'Do I frighten you? Are you afraid I'll exact my revenge?'

She flinched and her face lost all its colour. 'It was a long time ago. I was eighteen years old.'

Young. Scared. *Panicking like mad...*

'And that makes it all OK?'

Guilt stabbed her hard. 'I'm sorry if I— I didn't mean to—' She broke off and he lifted an eyebrow questioningly.

'You didn't mean to what, Jules?' His tone was conversational. 'Leave me standing at the altar without a word of explanation, wondering what the hell had happened to you?'

The picture he painted was so vivid that she closed her eyes briefly in an attempt to block it out, mortified by how he must have felt. 'I'm so sorry,' she whispered. 'What must everyone have thought? All the guests—'

'Do you really think I gave a damn about the guests?' His hand dropped to his side and he gave a frown. 'I wasn't interested in the guests and I never was. I was only ever interested in us. In you.'

She licked dry lips. 'I just couldn't do it.' Her breathing was shallow. 'It was all wrong. What we were doing was wrong.'

'Getting married?' His gaze dropped to her mouth and lingered. 'I don't think so, sweetheart. But I agree that the timing was wrong.'

'Not just the timing. Everything!' Juliet stepped back from him, wishing he hadn't called her 'sweetheart' in that lazy, teasing way that she remembered so well. 'It never would have worked. We were getting married for all the wrong reasons.'

Finn stilled. 'You tell me why you think we were getting married,' he probed gently, his gaze curiously intent. 'Tell me, Jules. I want to know.'

Pain twisted inside her and she stared up at him in anguish, her hands clenched by her sides. 'You *know* why.'

He stared at her thoughtfully. 'I know why *I* was getting married,' he said evenly, 'but I'd like to hear what *your* reasons were.'

She bit her lip and tears clogged her throat. 'I can't talk about it. And I don't know why you're forcing me to. It's all irrelevant now.'

'We're talking about it because it's time you stopped running. You've run for ten years and you're going to keep running unless you stand still and face what happened.' He gave a crooked smile and brushed his fingers over her cheek in a gesture of comfort that made her want to sob. 'My cowardly Jules. On the outside you're so gutsy and feisty. You'll climb to the top of Everest if you get the chance, you'll sail the roughest seas and you'll raft down wild rivers. But when it comes to relationships you run a mile every time. And as for marriage…'

'Finn—'

'It takes real courage to commit to one person for a lifetime, and you couldn't do it, could you?'

'Neither could you.'

'No?' His tone was steady. 'So why was I waiting in the church that cold winter morning with the ring in my pocket? I waited and waited, but you didn't show up.'

She curled her fingers into her palms. 'I did us both a favour. You didn't really want to marry me, you know you didn't.'

'Then why was I standing in the church?'

'We both know why.' Her eyes filled with pain, her heart twisted in agony and for a moment she just couldn't speak.

'You're not going to say it, are you? So I'm going to have to say it for both of us.' He stood in front of her, his eyes on her face, his broad shoulders suddenly tense. 'You thought I was standing in the church because of our baby. You thought I was marrying you because you were having our baby.'

Pain sliced through her and she took another step backwards, her knees shaking. 'Don't mention the baby. I don't ever want to talk about the baby.'

How could it hurt so much?

After all this time, how could it cause so much pain?

With a soft curse he grabbed her shoulders and gave her a gentle shake. 'It happened, Jules, and we never talked about it because you ran.'

And he hadn't followed her.

His fingers bit into her shoulders and his words bit into her heart. 'There wasn't a baby, Finn. I lost the baby. Remember? I lost it at three months, precisely two weeks before the wedding. It happens to loads of women. You're a doctor, you know that. It's normal. Just another one of nature's nasty little surprises. And I don't want to talk about it. I don't want to do this.' She wriggled out of his grip and backed away from him. 'I'm going back inside and tomorrow, when we meet in public, I want you to pretend that you never met me before this expedition. I want us to act like we're strangers, because that's what we are now. I don't ever want to talk about the past again and I certainly don't ever want to talk about our baby. And don't try and guilt-trip me. I did us both a favour by not turning up that day and you know it.'

Heart pounding, her mouth dry, she stared at him for a moment and then turned and ran back into the safety of the lodge.

She was the only woman he'd ever loved.

And she was still running from him.

What the hell had he been thinking? Finn closed his eyes and silently cursed his lack of tact. He shouldn't have mentioned the baby. Or the wedding that never was. He hadn't planned to mention any of it but when he'd seen Simon with his hands on her he'd been driven by a primitive urge to protect and claim his woman.

Which was ridiculous, he reminded himself with a humourless laugh, because Juliet Adams wasn't his woman. She wasn't anyone's woman.

She was wild and restless and difficult to handle and he knew that better than anyone. She'd been the same as a child and she hadn't changed when she'd grown into a woman. She kept her relationships superficial and she kept them short.

Juliet wasn't anyone's idea of a sure thing.

And he knew why. *He understood why.* His mouth tightened into a grim line. She'd lost her father and her brother in these mountains and she guarded her heart so carefully that no one was able to get close.

He knew all that.

But even with his experience of handling her, he'd managed to get it all wrong.

He retraced their conversation in his head and muttered a soft curse. Hadn't he learned anything over the years? Cornering her never worked. She always panicked and backed away. She always ran.

She was utterly terrified of being pinned down, tied to one place or one person.

In fact, given the sort of person she was, it was amazing that he'd even managed to get an engagement ring on her finger.

And if she hadn't been pregnant, she wouldn't have said yes.

With a sigh of exasperation he turned away from the lodge and took a few deep breaths of the freezing air.

Ten years.

It had been ten years since they'd last met and seeing her again had stirred up emotions that he'd kept well and truly buried.

But now he'd opened the box. He stared out into the darkness, in the direction of Everest.

Climbing that mountain required the utmost concentration. Eight thousand eight hundred and forty-eight metres above sea level was no place for emotional entanglements and complications.

And yet how could they avoid it?

They were here now and, as far as he was concerned, her trick of pretending they didn't know each other just made the situation even worse.

It was typical Jules, he thought to himself. Vintage Jules. Stick your head in the sand or, in her case, travel to the ends of the earth and the problem just might not catch up with you. Climb high enough, drive fast enough and you just might leave it behind.

Whereas he—he always preferred to face the enemy. Deal with issues, no matter how difficult or uncomfortable.

Finn's jaw hardened. He'd seen the look in her eyes and knew that her feelings were as raw as ever. She wasn't indifferent—she was frightened. And deep down he'd always known that.

He should have tracked her down sooner. The moment he'd realised that she wasn't going to show up for her own wedding, he should have gone after her and forced her to talk. And he'd intended to, of course, but then circumstances had changed everything.

Her brother had died. His best friend. Climbing Everest.

And because of the pain and the grief and the muddle of their lives, he'd let her go.

Finn ran a hand over the back of his neck and admitted to himself that letting her go had been the biggest mistake of all. He'd let her go because dealing with her had been like handling an explosive substance. He'd let her go because he'd convinced himself that she didn't love him enough to make the commitment that he'd demanded of her. But most of all he'd let her go because he'd come to realise that there were some things you just couldn't hold onto. Some creatures that just couldn't be tamed.

And Juliet Adams was one of them.

But now she was back here, in this most dangerous of places, and he knew instinctively that she wasn't climbing for herself.

She was climbing for her brother.

And that made the situation more dangerous than ever.

CHAPTER FOUR

Namche Bazaar, Nepal, 3450 metres above sea level

BREAKFAST was a quiet affair.

After the trauma of the night before, Juliet would have preferred to have a day on her own to think and get her head together, but she had a responsibility towards the trekkers, particularly as they were now at a height where altitude could become a problem.

Her head throbbed and her eyes felt gritty and heavy from lack of sleep. She wished she could blame it on the altitude but she knew that the way she was feeling had nothing to do with where she was and everything to do with Finn.

Sally also seemed tired and the guys said very little. Diane didn't make an appearance at all.

'Is she all right?' Juliet drank a large glass of water and wondered if there was trouble brewing.

'I think so. Just tired. She's not the only one. I wish I'd opted to stay in bed and skip breakfast. I'm not hungry anyway.' Sally dropped her fork, leaving her omelette untouched, and Juliet put a sympathetic hand on her arm.

'It's normal to feel a bit drained after a day like yesterday.' Her tone was gentle. 'You're doing really, really well but we'll see how you go today.' His eyes narrowed as she scanned the two men.

'How did you sleep?'

Gary took another sip of tea. 'Fine.'

Simon didn't meet her eyes. 'Great.'

He hadn't apologised for his behaviour the night before and Juliet could hardly remember it now. All she could think about was what had happened afterwards with Finn.

For ten years she'd engineered it so that their paths didn't cross.

For ten years she'd avoided talking about what had happened between them.

And now they were both here, in the same place at the same time, and he was refusing to keep his distance.

She felt panic flutter inside her like a wild bird.

He'd looked at her in that steady, determined way that made it difficult to breathe. And maybe she did feel a little guilty that she'd left him standing in the church, but she'd done them both a favour. Couldn't he see that?

Surely he should be thanking her for saving him from making the biggest mistake of his life?

Next time they were on their own she'd talk to him, get him to admit that he had only wanted to marry her because she'd been pregnant. Then they could both move on.

Their past would finally be behind them.

Decision made, she turned to Sally. 'Did you have a bad night?'

Sally managed a smile and a shrug. 'Oh, you know—strange bed and all that jazz.'

In other words, she hadn't slept at all. 'Difficulty in sleeping is common at altitude.' Juliet drank more water herself. 'Do you have a headache?'

Sally pulled a face. 'Doesn't one always after a bad night?'

Juliet studied her for a moment. 'Possibly,' she said quietly, and made a mental note to check on the other girl later. 'We're going to stay here today. I recommend that you join Neil on a walk. He'll take you higher up and then you'll come back down here to sleep. It's an important part of the acclimatisation process. Climb high, sleep low.'

Sally's face fell. 'We're going higher?'

'And then coming back down again. It will help your body adjust to the altitude. But if you don't feel well enough, stay here and rest.'

And if Sally's symptoms hadn't improved, she'd be sending her back down the valley. She wasn't risking anyone's health.

Sally breathed out and then gave a smile. 'No. I want to climb with Neil. He was telling me last night that the views of Everest are fantastic from the walk he has planned.'

Juliet looked at the two men and Simon shrugged. 'I'm in. No problem.'

But he looked tired and there was something about his eyes that made Juliet wonder if he was suffering. Merely the amount he'd drunk should have been enough to give him a headache, without the altitude.

She'd have to warn Neil to keep a close eye on him. She finished her water, picked at her omelette and then rose from the table. She wanted to be away from the dining room before Finn turned up.

The next time they talked was going to be at a place of her choosing.

Juliet collected her day pack and made her way out of the lodge, intending to explore, when there was a shout behind her and Simon caught up with her.

'Hey.' He ran a hand through his hair and hesitated, obviously searching for the right words. Then he spread his hands and gave a boyish shrug. 'I'm sorry about last night. I behaved like an idiot. Too much fresh air and chang beer.'

Surprised and touched by the unexpected admission, she smiled. 'Forget it. But alcohol and altitude don't tend to mix. You might want to remember that.'

'Don't worry.' He gave a rueful smile. 'I've well and truly got that message. My head feels as though Everest is sitting on it.'

Suddenly he seemed to have dropped the macho act and she found herself warming to him.

'Just how bad is that headache of yours?'

He pulled a face and lifted a hand to keep her at a distance. 'It's just a hangover, Doc. It'll be fine. I don't need any lotions or potions.'

'Well, if it isn't fine, you need to let me know. An alcohol headache will clear up. An altitude one doesn't.'

He nodded. 'I'll get some exercise with Neil today. See if it clears. Oh, and, Dr Adams...' He gave her a sheepish grin as he turned back towards the lodge. 'I still think you're sexy as hell, so if you ever change you mind...'

She smiled, knowing that this time there was nothing threatening about the comment. 'I won't change my mind.'

He gave a shrug. 'I suppose I can hardly blame you. Finn McEwan is unfair competition. There aren't many guys who could compete with him.'

Her smile faded and she stood still as Simon strolled back inside the lodge.

Was that what he thought? That she was interested in Finn?

She bit back a groan. That was all she needed. Simon suggesting that there was something going on between her and Finn.

She'd wanted their past to remain a secret, didn't want anyone speculating on their relationship because they didn't have one any more. And they never would again. It had all been a dreadful mistake, one that had escalated out of control.

She wasn't the right woman for Finn.

She wasn't the right woman for any man.

The headaches cleared, Diane felt better after a rest day and over the next few days they slowly trekked upward, gaining altitude, closing the distance to Everest Base Camp.

They walked to the village of Tengboche with its famous monastery and spent the night camping then trekked up to Pheriche where they had another day acclimatising.

Pheriche was home to a medical clinic run by the Himalayan Rescue Association, staffed by volunteer Western doctors. Juliet had worked there a few years before and she knew that Finn had also spent time there. It had been established to treat and advise trekkers on altitude sickness but they also provided a medical service for the local population.

Sally was coughing badly, as was Gary, and Juliet examined them both to exclude the possibility of chest infection.

'It's not infection,' she said finally, pulling the stethoscope out of her ears. 'It's high-altitude cough. The relative humidity up here is very low,' she explained. 'The air is dry and cold and that irritates the respiratory tract. On top of that you're breathing more to make up for the lack of oxygen, and mouth breathing and increased ventilation all dry the respiratory mucosa. Climbers often wear masks so that the air they breathe is warmed and moisturised. You can try covering your mouth with a scarf but this high up it can just make you feel suffocated.'

Sally coughed again. 'So it's just one of the benefits of taking a holiday in this part of the world.'

'Mountain air isn't always that healthy when you climb this high.' Juliet put her stethoscope away. 'But it's a lot more exciting than lying on a beach in the Caribbean. I'll give you some throat lozenges to suck, they sometimes help.'

Diane was complaining of headaches again and Juliet suspected that the two guys were also feeling the altitude, although they refused to admit as much when questioned.

'Are we falling behind our schedule?' It was Simon who asked the question and Juliet shook her head.

'We always work "spare" days into our itinerary. It means that we're able to spend extra time acclimatising when we need to.' She zipped up the bag that contained her medical kit. 'The increased incidence of altitude sickness among trekkers is largely among those who come in big organised groups. Everyone walks at the same pace and there's no scope for flexibility. That's why we keep our groups small. That way we can accommodate each individual.'

'So what happens tomorrow?'

'All being well, we'll make our way up to Lobuje. And, believe me…' she scraped her hair away from her face '…we won't be lingering.'

Lobuje, Nepal, 4930 metres above sea level

They left behind any trace of green and moved slowly up the boulder-strewn valley into the biting wind and eventually arrived at the lower end of the Khumbu glacier.

Here the air was thinner, the outlook barren and part of the trail towards Base Camp was still buried under winter snow.

The yaks, struggling under their heavy loads, sank to their bellies in the deep snow while their drivers urged them on.

Lobuje consisted of nothing more than a few tea-houses and huts. It was cold, high and bleak.

'This place is seriously filthy,' Juliet warned as they picked their way through stinking, muddy water to a place above the huts where the Sherpas had chosen to establish their camp. 'I think people are too weighed down by the altitude by the time they reach here to be bothered by a little thing like hygiene. We'll be staying here for as short a time as possible.'

She was intending to minimise the time they spent in Lobuje in the hope that she could move all the trekkers on before they caught something nasty.

The cook was melting snow ready for boiling but she had no confidence that they would be able to stay long in the place without picking up an infection.

They ate dinner and retired to their tents, but during the night she was woken by Sally, who had been struck down by a nasty attack of diarrhoea and vomiting.

'It's nothing to worry about. It's pretty much to be expected in this part of the world,' Juliet said sympathetically as she helped Sally back to her tent and encouraged her to drink. 'I could give you some Imodium but, to be honest, it's best to get it out of your system. We'll see how you go.'

Sally was ill for most of the night but the next morning she was feeling weak but decidedly better and announced that she was more than ready for the final trek up to Base Camp.

Unfortunately for the two men it was a different story.

'Your trekkers have altitude sickness.' Finn strolled over to Juliet as she finished her tea and she scrambled to her feet, caught off guard by his sudden appearance, the rest of the liquid spilling over her feet as her shaking fingers lost their grip on the mug. She hadn't known Finn was in Lobuje.

Her heart gave a lurch and her immediate thought was that he was the best-looking thing in the place. His trousers had moulded themselves to the hard muscle of his thighs and his hair gleamed dark in the wintry sunlight. He looked strong and tough and very much in control, a man totally at one with his surroundings. But Finn had always been at home in the mountains.

'I didn't know you were here.'

'Did you think you'd lost me?' He gave a slight smile. 'You could say I'm on your heels, Jules.' He glanced up the valley and then back towards her, a challenging gleam in his dark eyes. 'And you're running into a dead end.'

Her heart gave another thump. What exactly did he mean by that?

Was he talking about the walk or something else entirely?

'Finn—'

'Where are you going to run to once we reach Base Camp?' His tone was pleasant. 'To the summit?'

'I'm not running.'

'You're avoiding me.'

'I'm not avoiding you.'

'So could we manage to have a conversation without you leaving before the end?'

'Finn.' She swallowed, and her hand shook slightly as she pushed the hair away from her face. 'All right—you want to do this now? Let's do this now. Maybe I do owe you an apology for leaving you at the church and I'm certainly sorry for embarrassing you, but I'm not sorry that we didn't get married. I did us both a favour, Finn.'

'How's that?'

She stared at him in exasperation. 'You didn't want to get married any more than I did, but you were too much of a gentleman to do anything about it!'

A muscle flickered in his cheek and a strange expression flickered across his handsome face. His dark eyes dropped to her mouth and lingered there for endless seconds. 'You thought I was marrying you because I was too much of a gentleman to break it off?'

'Of course!' She looked away from him, unsettled by the look in his eyes. She wished he wouldn't keep looking at her mouth. It made her think what it was like to kiss him and she didn't want to remember that right now. *She was sure there wasn't a man alive who kissed like Finn.* 'You offered to marry me because I was pregnant, and when I lost the baby I did what was right for both of us. I did us both a massive favour.'

His eyes lifted to hers, his expression thoughtful. 'Do you truly believe that?'

'It's the truth, Finn.'

'*Your* version of the truth,' he said slowly, stepping closer to her. 'Now you can hear *my* version.'

She stared at him. 'Our versions are both the same, it's just that you're afraid to admit it.'

'Uh-huh.' He shook his head slowly. 'I'm not the one who's scared around here. You're the one who's afraid, Jules, of your own feelings.'

She lifted her chin and her eyes sparked. 'I'm not afraid of anything, Finn.' She chewed her lip. 'Except flying.'

He was silent for a long second and then he slid a hand across her cheek and into her hair, forcing her to look at him. 'You're afraid of your own emotions, sweetheart, that's what you're afraid of. I was marrying you because I loved you,' he said softly. 'I've always loved you. And deep down you knew that. And it frightened the life out of you.'

She stared at him, stunned, and her heart stumbled and took off at a frantic pace. 'That isn't true.'

It couldn't be. He hadn't followed her. He hadn't come after her.

'I know it's scary for you to hear that, but it is true,' Finn said quietly, his dark eyes steady on hers. 'I should have told you sooner but you were young and always so jumpy and commitment-shy that I didn't want to crowd you. I was biding my time. Playing a waiting game.' He gave a wry, self-deprecating smile. 'Unfortunately I wasn't that great at waiting, was I?'

She flushed as explicit, erotic memories flashed into her brain. 'That was my fault, too,' she mumbled. 'You always tried to keep your distance from me. I seduced you.' *She'd been desperate for him.* She tried to move her face away from his hand but he held her firm.

'Hardly. I'd been holding back for so long I was on the edge. I always promised myself I wouldn't touch you until you were eighteen.' He gave her a lazy, sexy smile. 'I made it by about two hours if my recollection is correct.'

Her whole body heated and throbbed. 'So…' Juliet's green eyes were fiery as she glared at him. 'We had sex. That doesn't mean anything. Plenty of people have sex without getting married.'

His firm mouth moved in the glimmer of a smile. 'You were a virgin, Jules, so don't make it sound like a casual encounter. We both know it meant more than that.'

Her heart was thudding so hard she wondered that he couldn't hear it. 'Every woman has a first—it's not that big a deal.'

'Ouch.' His eyes gleamed with lazy amusement. 'It's a good job my ego is robust. *Not that big a deal?*' his eyes dropped to her mouth again. 'Do you want me to describe it to you? Jog your memory?'

'No!' She jerked away from him, suddenly unable to breathe. 'No, I do not. And I don't understand what this is about. Why are you doing this? It's all over.'

'It's still there between us and it always will be until you learn to talk about it and stop avoiding things that frighten you,' he said calmly, lifting a hand and smoothing a strand of blonde hair away from her face.

'I want you to admit that I loved you. And I want you to admit that you loved me, too.'

Her legs shook and she stared at him, her breath coming in short rapid pants. 'I didn't love you. I'm sorry, but I didn't love you, Finn.'

He reached out a hand and hauled her back against him, his mouth only inches from hers. 'Remember that night we made love for the first time, Jules?' His voice was husky and masculine. 'You sobbed and cried and clung to me.'

She could hardly breathe. All she could feel was the hard press of his powerful body against hers and the bite of his fingers. 'So, you're a good lover.'

'You think this was about bedroom technique?'

'Finn—'

'You're forgetting that I know you better than anyone, Juliet,' he said quietly. 'And I always have. I've known you since you were four years old. I knew you loved me but I also knew you were panicking about the wedding. I could see it in your eyes and feel it in your kiss. You were so afraid you were all jammed up inside. I was waiting for you to talk to me about it. I thought you trusted me that much.'

Guilt twisted inside her.

'Frankly I was amazed that you didn't break it off and run as soon as you lost the baby. I should have known you would never make it to the church.'

'I didn't plan it,' she said desperately, trying to make him understand. *But how could she explain something that she didn't understand herself?* 'I just woke up and—' She broke off, her heart pounding with the memory. 'I just knew I couldn't do it. I couldn't do it, and I'm sorry.'

She was breathing rapidly and he stood watching her, his dark eyes steady on her face.

'You owe me more than a guilty "sorry", Jules. You owe me a proper explanation. A conversation where you don't run away before the end of it. I want you to talk about what happened and I want you to talk about how you felt. I want you to open up.'

'No.'

'Yes.' He gave a harsh laugh. 'Have you any idea how contrary you are? You're the only woman I know who doesn't talk about her feelings and the only woman I know who isn't obsessed with marriage and settling down.'

She backed away from him, her eyes wide and her cheeks flushed. 'I don't want to settle down.'

'I know that.' His voice was patient, as if he were speaking to a wild animal on the brink of flight. 'I think you gave me a clue when you fled from our wedding.'

'Dr Adams? Juliet?' Sally called across to her from the other tent and Finn gave a wry smile and a resigned shrug.

'You'd better go and deal with your sick trekkers, Dr Adams. But don't think this is the end of the conversation. We've barely started.'

'Trekkers?' Her voice croaky, Juliet turned her head and blinked, realising that she'd totally forgotten the existence of the trekkers until this moment. All she'd been aware of had been Finn. 'One of them is ill?"

'Both of them.' Finn stooped and picked up her medical bag. 'I expect you're going to be needing this.'

Juliet tried to concentrate—tried to push the dark, swirling thoughts out of her mind. 'All right, we'll talk.' He wasn't going to take no for an answer and, anyway, maybe talking would help. They could end it, once and for all. 'But not here, and not now. It isn't the right place.'

He pushed the bag into her shaking hands and gave a crooked smile that was both mocking and sexy. 'We're at five thousand metres, sweetheart. Just what constitutes "the right place"? Everest isn't exactly a good place for a formal date.'

'I don't want a date.' Her heart thumped. She couldn't believe she was saying that. There'd been a time when a date with Finn had been all she'd dreamed of. 'But I know I owe you an apology.'

His gaze dropped to her mouth. 'You owe me the truth, Jules,' he said softly, 'and that's what I want from you. I want to you to admit that you loved me, and that you ran from me because you were scared of your own feelings. And mine. You're terrified of being hurt, and that's why you run.'

She stared at him, frozen and poised in terror, like a deer who has spotted danger.

But through her building panic she was aware of the sudden flare of heat low in her pelvis. The chemistry between them was so powerful that it took her breath away.

But it wasn't love.

It had never been love, she told herself frantically.

Finn was a staggeringly handsome, interesting, charismatic man and there wasn't a woman on the planet who wouldn't respond to the attentions of a man like him.

It wasn't love.

'I think we have a different view of the past,' she said shakily, clutching her medical bag to her chest like a barrier. 'And I don't see the point in talking about it. We're both going to have other things on our mind once we reach Base Camp.'

'You think so?' He placed a finger over her mouth to stop her talking. 'Go and see to your trekkers, Dr Adams. We'll continue this conversation later.'

She didn't want to carry on the conversation later, she thought frantically. She wasn't in love with him and she never had been.

It had been friendship. And a strong physical attraction, certainly—*but love?*

No, no, and *no!*

Juliet changed the subject quickly. 'How do you know they're ill?'

She walked towards the tents and Finn stayed by her side.

'I heard them being sick,' Finn said dryly, 'so that's a clue. Could be a stomach bug, of course, but given the rest of the facts I very much doubt it. They overdid it yesterday and they've been complaining on and off about headaches.' He cast a speculative look in her direction. 'You're breathless, Dr Adams. Are you sure that the altitude isn't affecting you?'

He knew exactly what was troubling her but she wasn't going to give him the satisfaction of admitting just how much he'd unsettled her.

'We're very high up here,' she hedged, dragging her eyes away from the dark stubble on his jaw. He looked rough, masculine and sexier than any man had a right to be at this altitude. 'It's normal to breathe more rapidly, as you well know.'

His gaze rested on her face. 'I also know that you're perfectly accustomed to walking at altitude. Is my presence here bothering you, Jules?'

Her breathing stopped altogether. 'Why would your presence worry me?' She tried to sound nonchalant and his gaze dropped to her mouth and then lifted again.

'I can think of a number of reasons. Would you like me to list them?'

'No. No, I definitely wouldn't. And you being here doesn't bother me,' she lied, 'and I'm breathless because we're high up, there isn't enough oxygen in the air and I walked too fast yesterday. And now, if you'll excuse me, I need to see to my trekkers. They're my responsibility until we reach Base Camp.'

After that another trek leader would escort them back down the trail to Lukla, where they would catch a flight back to Kathmandu.

'Could be the food.'

'Could be,' Finn conceded, 'but then there's the

headaches they mentioned. If you want my opinion, your trekkers have AMS.'

Acute mountain sickness.

Juliet hoped that wasn't the case or they'd be descending, because the only cure was to climb down to a lower altitude in order to let the body recover.

She glanced around her with an expression of distaste. 'The sickness could just be this place. It's unhygienic and generally disgusting.'

'Not exactly the Ritz,' Finn agreed, pausing outside the tent and lifting the flap. 'How are you men doing now?'

There was a grunt of acknowledgement and Gary stuck his head out of the tent, his eyes half-shut.

'I've stopped being sick but I feel dreadful and my head is being hit by a hammer.'

Juliet's heart sank. 'It doesn't have to be altitude sickness. There are plenty of causes for a headache. Did you sleep last night?'

He shook his head. 'First it was my stomach, then my head, then my stomach again. Sleep didn't get a look-in.'

Juliet examined him as best she could in the circumstances. 'He has a mild tachycardia and his temperature is slightly raised,' she muttered to Finn as she pulled her stethoscope out of her bag and listened to Gary's chest. 'That sounds clear.'

She sat back on her heels and looked at the trekker. 'You walked quite fast yesterday. Did you drink alcohol last night?'

She was running through all the possibilities, but Gary pulled a face and shook his head. 'Didn't feel well enough.'

'Did you drink much fluid at all?' Could he be suffering from dehydration? It was certainly possible. 'Are you passing urine frequently?'

Gary shook his head. 'Not much.'

Faced with a difficult decision, Juliet looked at Finn. 'What do you think?' Whatever else she thought of him, she knew him to be a highly skilled doctor and she valued his opinion. 'It isn't cut and dried, is it?'

'AMS never is,' he said dryly, 'but you know the rules as well as I do.'

Juliet bit her lip and dropped her stethoscope back into her bag. 'You think he should descend?'

'I think it's always best to be conservative,' Finn advised, a sympathetic expression on his handsome face. 'A difficult decision, I know, but the truth is he needs to go down. A drop in altitude should solve the problem. If it doesn't then we're looking at something else entirely.'

By now Neil had joined them. 'I'm not feeling that well myself,' he admitted as he listened to them talking and caught the drift of the conversation, 'so I'm very happy to provide the escort. We'll go back down to Pheriche and then if he doesn't improve at least he can see the doctors in the clinic. He can wait for the rest of his party there and I'll climb back up in a few days and meet you at Base Camp when my pounding headache has gone.'

Juliet brushed her hair out of her eyes, suddenly feeling exhausted. 'You, too?'

Neil grinned and gave a boyish shrug. 'Me, too. Oh, how the mighty are fallen.'

Suddenly everyone seemed to be feeling the effects of altitude.

Juliet hesitated. Sending Gary back down the mountain seemed like the only solution but still it was hard to terminate someone's dreams. She knew that if Gary dropped down now, he wouldn't be climbing back up again. There wasn't sufficient time in the trekking programme to allow for a further ascent up the Khumbu glacier to Base Camp.

Gary glanced between them and then gave a resigned shrug. 'So I guess that's it for me. You can't see the summit from Base Camp anyway,' he muttered with surprising good humour. 'We've already had the best views of the mountain and frankly I feel so bad I couldn't face taking another step upwards if you offered me money. I'm actually not that bothered to be going down.'

He looked grim and while they were sitting there, debating the best course of action, he had to hurry away to be sick again.

'I'll give him something for the nausea and vomiting,' Juliet said finally, opening her bag again, 'and some aspirin for the headache. I'll give Neil some acetazolamide and dexamethasone in case he gets worse on the way down. How's Simon?'

Simon hadn't even emerged from the tent and was

lying on his side with his eyes closed. 'Don't tell me it's time to go,' he groaned. 'I haven't got the energy.'

'Send both of them down,' Finn said immediately, a frown in his eyes. 'This is probably a result of both of them overdoing it on the trail over the past few days. They're exhausted and that tends to contribute to the development of AMS.'

Juliet sat back on her heels and sighed. 'I tried telling them to slow down.'

'I wish I'd listened.' Simon kept his eyes closed. 'Your story of the hare and the tortoise doesn't seem so stupid now.'

Juliet gave a sympathetic smile. 'AMS can hit anyone. It isn't anything to do with fitness and it's entirely unpredictable.'

'Experienced mountaineers can suddenly be struck by AMS,' Finn confirmed, obviously prepared to be conciliatory despite the other man's behaviour earlier in the trek. 'You can come back another year. Everest isn't going anywhere.'

Juliet looked at Finn, scanning his strong, masculine features, and wondered whether Finn had ever known weakness in his life.

It was still only a little after six o'clock in the morning but both girls were already up and dressed, ready for action and more than a little disappointed that the two men were going to be turning back.

'We're virtually there,' Sally pointed out, visibly disappointed. 'Another day's trek up the valley—'

'Which takes you even higher and could be one day

too many,' Finn said with a shake of his head. 'They need to go down. How are you feeling?'

The two girls conferred and decided that they really wanted to carry on up to Base Camp.

'In that case, we should get moving,' Juliet said decisively, glancing around her with an expression of distaste. 'This place is a well of disease and we don't want to linger here for longer than is necessary or we'll all be picking up something horrible. Neil? Will you be OK?'

Neil frowned. 'Yes, but I don't like the thought of you going up there alone.'

'I'm not alone,' Juliet pointed out in a dry tone. 'I'm surrounded by Sherpas, yaks and enough supplies to keep me going for several months.'

Finn lifted his rucksack onto his back. 'I'll trek with them,' he told Neil, 'which leaves you free to go back down to Pheriche.'

Juliet bristled. 'I don't need an escort.'

'Well, you've got one.' Finn's tone was cool and steady. 'If something happens to Sally or Diane, you're going to need help.'

They looked at each other and something passed between them.

Juliet wanted to say no but she knew that to do so would trigger questions from Neil. And she didn't want to answer those questions. She didn't want anyone knowing about her relationship with Finn.

It was complicated enough dealing with her feelings without having an audience speculating and observing her every move.

'Fine.' She managed a casual smile. 'We'll trek together.'

She consoled herself with the thought that it was only a day's walk to Base Camp, and once there she and Finn would be far too busy with their respective expedition members to spend any time with each other. They would have one conversation, just to clear the air, and that would be it.

They set off after breakfast and began the long, slow trek up to Base Camp to the musical accompaniment of yak bells and the calls of the Sherpas as they encouraged the animals over the less than inviting terrain.

They were walking at the bottom of the glacier now, over gravel and past huge icebergs and boulders that had been carried down the ice stream.

Beneath their feet the glacier rumbled as subterranean streams, formed from melted ice, found a way down the mountain.

They trudged slowly upwards, following the piles of stones that had been left by the Sherpas to mark the route.

Everyone was feeling the effects of the altitude. The girls were quiet and Sally complained of feeling dizzy, but both seemed determined to make it to their final destination before turning back.

They followed the line of the glacier as it turned to the east and finally the grey, almost lunar landscape gave way to a splash of colour. A city of brightly coloured tents, all bearing different logos, lay ahead of them. A small, man-made village which would stay on the glacier for the time it took the various expeditions to make their attempts on the mountain.

They had reached Everest Base Camp.

CHAPTER FIVE

Everest Base Camp, 5400 metres above sea level

CLIMBING Everest demanded a gradual process of acclimatisation. Four camps were established between Base Camp and the summit, and climbers moved between them over a period of weeks, allowing their bodies to make adjustments to the altitude, increasing their chances of reaching the summit at the point when the weather might permit such an attempt.

But, for now, Base Camp was home.

There were more than four hundred people, a mixture of climbers and Sherpas, on the mountain that season, and Base Camp was busy, a village of brightly coloured tents perched on some of the most inhospitable terrain on earth.

The tents for Everest expeditions were clustered together on a prime spot, near a water supply and away from the toilet.

Sally and Diane were so exhausted they could barely drag themselves the final few metres towards the tents, the walk having left them wheezing and breathless.

'There's no air up here. I feel as though I'm suffocating,' Sally gasped as she sank onto a boulder to rest. Juliet nodded, feeling the lack of oxygen herself.

'Your lungs have to work twice as hard to take in the oxygen they need because air pressure here is only half what it is at sea level.'

The plan was that the trekkers would spend a night at Base Camp before beginning the trek back down the valley and home.

Juliet had barely had time to take the rucksack off her back and greet Billy, the expedition leader, when their Base Camp manager hurried towards her.

'There's been an accident in the icefall. A Swedish climber didn't clip on properly and he fell into a crevasse as they were descending. He's broken his ankle and they think he's developing frostbite. There are some American climbers at Camp I who are helping him, but they need medical advice and were wondering who would help. I've asked Finn to give us a hand, too.'

Juliet looked up at the huge, tumbling cascade of broken ice and snow that formed the Khumbu Icefall. It must rank as one of the most inhospitable places on earth to sustain an injury of any sort.

Constantly shifting and moving, this section of Everest formed the most technically demanding and dangerous section of the climb. Successful negotiation of the icefall meant passing under numerous seracs, sections of ice as large as tower blocks, that could crash down without warning in an avalanche, burying anyone crossing beneath. The route up to Camp 1 also meant passing over deep crevasses by means of ladders roped together. As the sun melted the snow and ice the ladders sometimes shifted and fell deep into the bowels of the mountain.

Climbers tackling the icefall did so early in the day, before the sun hit the slopes and increased the risk still further.

At the beginning of the season, Sherpas and climbers anchored a static line of rope from the bottom of the icefall to the top, and each climber was expected to tether themselves to this fixed line.

Clearly the injured climber had neglected to secure himself to the fixed rope.

'Any other injuries? Head injury?' Despite her own lack of physical reserves, Juliet immediately snapped into doctor mode. 'What have they done to the ankle?'

She knew that if they didn't splint the damaged limb carefully, there could be permanent damage.

'We've got them on the radio in the tent.'

Still gasping for air, Juliet walked as quickly as she could to the tent so that she could issue advice over the radio, worrying about the prospect of delivering medical care to a potentially seriously injured climber when she hadn't even had time to unpack her supplies.

She sank down onto a crate that was serving as a seat and took the radio. 'What was he doing in the icefall this late in the day, anyway?'

The sun on the ice would have made it lethal. That was why so much climbing at high altitude took place in darkness with the aid of flashlights. The conditions were more stable in the chill of the night.

'He was on his way down when he fell. Apparently it took the Americans ages to get him out because he wasn't roped up.'

'He was lucky that they managed to get him out at all,' Finn muttered as he joined them in the tent. 'And what was he doing up there in the icefall this early in the season? Most of the teams haven't even got their gear sorted out yet.'

'Obviously wanted to steal a march on everyone else,' Billy said wearily, handing Juliet the radio. 'It's all yours. There are two American climbers helping them out, but they're nervous about their first-aid abilities. I think they're worried that they've missed an injury. He fell a long way, apparently.'

Finn unzipped his jacket. 'How the hell did they get him out?'

'Landed on a ledge and they managed to get a rope down to him. From what I can gather, it was a mixture of him climbing the ice wall and them pulling from the top.'

'It's early in the season for accidents like that.'

Aware that Sally had joined her in the tent and was slumped on the floor, watching and listening, Juliet lifted the radio and spoke to the climbers who were dealing with the injured man.

After a series of questions she was able to ascertain

that the climber was conscious and lucid but had injured his ankle and lost his boot.

'Lost his boot?' Juliet stared incredulously at the radio for a moment, wondering if she'd misheard. 'How can he have lost his boot?'

The radio crackled to life and the American climber who was co-ordinating the rescue from the icefall explained that the Swedish man had insisted on removing the boot and had then let it fall into a crevasse.

'Seems pretty odd behaviour.' Finn McEwan sat down beside her, his broad shoulders tense. 'He could be suffering from HACE.'

Sally glanced between them. 'That's high-altitude cerebral oedema, yes?'

'It's a potentially fatal condition that results from the sudden increase in pressure in the brain due to swelling,' Juliet told her, 'but it's often characterised by confusion and an inability to think clearly. Maybe that's what happened to this guy.'

'It would certainly explain why he didn't clip onto the rope,' Finn said harshly, and Juliet looked at him, knowing exactly why he was so tense.

More skeletons in their cupboard.

Their eyes met and held.

For a moment the past threatened to swamp Juliet, but she pushed the darkness back and forced herself to concentrate on the present.

'We need to ask some questions and try and get a feel for what's going on. I can do that.' She hesitated and put a hand on his arm in silent communication. Not here. *Not now.* 'Why don't you try and find your tents?'

This wasn't the place to talk about the darkness she saw in his eyes.

A faint smile touched his hard mouth. 'Are you trying to get rid of me, Dr Adams?'

Aware that they had an interested audience, she shook her head and forced herself to look relaxed. 'Why would I try and get rid of you?' *Except that you're finding this situation every bit as hard as I am and I'm giving you a way out.* 'I just thought that since you've barely had a moment to check into this hotel, you might like some time to find your tents.'

'I already have and they're right next to yours.' His voice was soft and slightly mocking. 'So this trip is promising to be really, really cosy.'

'Oh.' His tents were right next to hers? Her hand dropped to her side and she stared at him in consternation.

'Something wrong, Dr Adams?' Finn lifted an eyebrow and she swallowed hard.

Yes. She didn't want his tents next to hers. She wanted them as far away as possible. *Preferably in a different mountain range.* She couldn't concentrate with him so close to her and she wouldn't be able to get on with her job if he was going to be breathing down her neck.

'I can handle this situation,' she said stiffly. 'I don't want to hold you up.'

He seemed to have completely recovered his composure.

'Well, that's the great thing about Base Camp. There isn't anywhere else I have to be,' he said in a lazy drawl. 'And you know as well as I do that, at this altitude, two heads are better than one. Even if one of them is stubborn and belongs to you.'

Billy gave a snort of amusement while Sally stared, wide-eyed and openly fascinated by the exchange.

Juliet gritted her teeth, knowing that she would be foolish to send him away. At this height, two heads *were* better than one and she knew that Finn was an excellent doctor. Promising herself that she'd deal with the emotional side of the problem later, she picked up the radio and asked a series of questions, satisfying herself that the first aid administered so far hadn't put the patient at further risk.

'The ankle is cold and they can't feel a pulse.' She looked at Finn. 'They need to try and straighten it.'

'They could do more damage.'

'But if they do nothing and his circulation is impaired, he could lose the foot.'

They were thinking aloud, going through the options, aware that they were dealing with people with limited medical skills operating in the harshest of conditions.

'It's hardly an ideal scenario.'

'Which is presumably why you enjoy hands-on high-altitude medicine,' Finn drawled lightly, pushing the radio towards her. 'You like working against the odds. This is medicine in the raw. Do nothing and the guy risks losing the foot. Or maybe even worse if they don't evacuate him before he dies of hypothermia.'

They looked at each other, each of them aware that out here in the wild the ideal scenario just didn't exist.

'They need to try and straighten the ankle,' she said finally, and Finn nodded.

'And then get him down. We'll deal with any frost-bite down here. So they need to splint that ankle. Are you going to talk them through it?'

She put her hand on the radio, wondering how on earth you talked someone through something so potentially serious.

She took a deep breath and spoke to the American climbers again, asking questions about the exact nature of the fracture, establishing as many facts as she could before giving instructions on splinting.

They made do with what they had—ice axes, ropes, sleeping pads—and Juliet calmly talked them through it, step by step, occasionally pausing to confer with Finn.

More questions revealed that the climber wasn't displaying symptoms of altitude sickness and had merely been careless in not clipping onto the fixed rope.

'Big mistake,' Juliet muttered, and Finn gave a wry smile.

'Easy enough for you to say because you're little. Try clipping onto a rope on the ground when you're over six foot. Believe me, the temptation not to bother if the ground looks safe is pretty strong.'

'I'm not little!' She sat up straight and glared at him. *'I'm not.'*

'You're five foot four,' he drawled softly, 'so you're hardly a giant.'

Deciding that this conversation was becoming all too personal, Juliet steered the subject back to how they were going to bring the patient down. 'Clearly he can't walk down. Can we send a team up with a stretcher?' She looked over her shoulder to where Billy was hovering in the entrance of the tent.

He pulled a face. 'Hard to say whether anyone will be prepared to brave the icefall for a guy who climbs on his own and can't be bothered to clip onto a rope, but I'll see what I can do.'

He left the tent and Juliet carried on talking to the climbers at Camp I. 'Can you feel pulses in his feet?'

'Yes.'

Satisfied that, for now at least, the injured climber's circulation wasn't compromised, Juliet turned her attention to the other risks. 'We need to keep his foot warm.'

The radio crackled. 'We've rigged something up. No worries.'

'Is he showing any other signs of injuries?'

'Not so far. He had new boots for this trip and they're too small. Hence the frostbite.'

Juliet sighed. 'Everest is not the place to break in a new pair of boots,' she explained to Sally, 'Tight footwear is one of the risk factors for frostbite.'

Finn walked back into the tent, carrying two steaming mugs of hot tea. 'Drink this.' He put a mug down beside her. 'You had a long, strenuous walk today. You need fluids and recovery time or you'll be the next patient.'

She took the tea gratefully. 'What's happening about the stretcher? Any luck?'

Finn hesitated. 'A few of us are going up now. It's going to take us hours so you get some rest. If I need you I'll radio.'

She felt her heart lurch. 'You're going into the ice-fall?'

He gave a wry smile. 'It's part of climbing Everest. You're going to be doing it, too.'

'But you've already walked today and—'

'Worrying about me, Jules?'

She licked dry lips. 'I just think maybe someone else should go.'

'Who, precisely?' His voice was weary as he walked back towards the entrance of the tent. 'Mountain rescue is a bit thin on the ground around here, as you well know. The Americans can't bring him down without a stretcher so we need to take one up.'

'All right.' Juliet shivered and glanced around her. 'I'll sleep here. That way I can speak to you on the radio if you encounter problems.'

She dosed fitfully and woke periodically to speak to the climbers on the radio to ascertain their position and talk through any new problems.

At 5 a.m. she was woken by loud bells as a large herd of yaks lumbered past, grunting and snorting as they carried their loads into the camp.

Billy stuck his head out of the tent. 'Base Camp is filling up,' he muttered, dragging his fingers through his dark hair and stifling a yawn. 'Just about all the expeditions will be here by the end of today. Are you all right?'

Juliet sat up, her head muzzy from lack of sleep and lack of oxygen. 'I'm just great,' she muttered, reaching for the radio again and checking the frequency.

'Don't bother,' Billy said. 'I can see them. They're just coming into Base Camp now.'

He went to meet them, and Finn and several other climbers arrived with the stretcher and the injured climber. The young Swedish man had been climbing alone and he was very sheepish and apologetic as Juliet redid his ankle and checked him over.

'You were very lucky,' she announced finally, as she finished splinting the ankle.

Finn walked back into the tent. 'The winds are too high for a helicopter evacuation so some of the Sherpas are going to walk down the valley with him. The doctor from the Spanish expedition is going down to pick up some supplies so he'll provide the escort.'

He looked exhausted and Juliet looked at him in concern. 'You need to go to bed.'

His gaze mocked her. 'Is that an invitation, Dr Adams?'

She blushed and turned her attention back to the injured climber, preparing him for evacuation. She knew that the most important thing was to stabilise his injuries and then get him off the mountain where he could be cared for properly.

In the end, the remaining trekkers left with them.

Sally and Diane were feeling the effects of altitude and were keen to rejoin Simon and Gary farther down the valley.

Having said her farewells, Juliet watched them go with mixed emotions. Now that the trekkers had left it was time to turn her attention to the serious job of climbing the mountain.

She returned to the medical tent and started unpacking her supplies. Everything had arrived safely and it was just a question of sorting it out into logical order so that she wouldn't be rummaging around if an emergency arose.

The sun had risen and Base Camp was surprisingly warm. Juliet stripped down to a thin top and her combat trousers, her baseball cap still pulled firmly over her eyes as she worked.

She checked and sorted, stacking equipment and deciding what she was going to carry with her when she made her first foray into the icefall in a few days' time.

'Still planning to climb, then?'

Finn stood in the entrance of the tent, his feet planted firmly apart, his shoulders blocking the light.

She felt a shiver of awareness and hated herself for it. She didn't want to react that way to him.

'Of course I'm climbing.' She stooped to unpack another crate. It was a way of not looking at him. 'You think I came all this way just to sit around and watch other people?'

'No. I don't think that.' He strolled into the tent. 'What are you doing here, Jules?'

'I'm living my life!' She shouted the words and he grabbed her shoulders and shook her.

'Are you? Or are you living his life? This is what he wanted, not you. Yes, you've climbed since you were small but every handhold you took was because he was driving you on, because it was what he wanted and expected. You didn't do it for you, Jules, you did it for him. And I think you're still doing it for him.'

Her eyes filled with tears. 'I had a great childhood.'

'He's dead, angel, and you can't bring him back. Climbing a mountain you don't want to climb isn't going to lessen the pain of losing him.'

'How do you know?'

'I just know that if you're searching for peace, you're not going to find it here in this windswept, desolate place.'

There was something in his tone that made her stop what she was doing. 'Look, Finn—' Juliet broke off and rose to her feet, choosing her words carefully. 'You don't need to worry about me.'

He folded his arms across his chest and a hint of a smile touched his hard mouth. 'You and I have unfinished business, Jules, and it isn't a good idea to climb this mountain with things left unsaid. Let's talk about what happened. All of it.'

She clasped her hands in front of her to stop them shaking. 'All right.' She accepted the inevitable. Perhaps if she had one conversation with him on his terms, he'd drop the subject. 'You keep saying that you were in love with me and yet that can't possibly be true.'

He lifted a dark eyebrow. 'Because?'

'Because you didn't come after me.' She curled her fingers into her palms. 'If you really loved me that much, why didn't you come after me?'

He inhaled sharply. 'Because what you needed most was space. You felt crowded and pressured. By the miscarriage and by me. You were panicking, Jules.'

She stared at him. 'You knew that?'

He gave a wry smile. 'Of course I knew that. So I made up my mind to give you that space. It made sense. But it all went wrong, didn't it?'

She bit her lip, her gaze tormented. 'I was due to go to Everest with Dan that spring, but I was so messed up after I lost the baby. And he died…' She closed her eyes briefly, feeling the guilt so acutely that she could hardly breathe. 'Because of me, he died.'

Finn swore softly and dragged her into his arms. 'He did *not* die because of you. You're not responsible for your brother's death.'

She looked up at him, her eyes swimming with pain. 'If I'd been there I could have made him more careful. I always did.'

Finn stroked the hair away from her face with a gentle hand. 'You couldn't have changed him. Dan was always wild.' He gave a wry smile. 'Even wilder than you.'

'He developed cerebral oedema up at Camp IV but no one recognised it.' Juliet pulled away from Finn, half talking to herself. 'They just thought he was being Dan. No one stopped him going higher.'

'It's easy to miss the signs. Up there in the Death Zone, you don't have energy for yourself, let alone anyone else. Your brain is slowly dying—everything becomes more difficult. Thinking, moving, co-ordinating your body. It's so easy for people to stand at sea level and judge us, but up there it's a different world. You know that, Jules. The body behaves differently and so does the brain.'

Juliet shivered.

The Death Zone.

The name given by climbers to the very extremes of altitude where the human body starts to deteriorate, eating away at its own muscle and bone in a desperate struggle for survival.

'If I'd been there, it might have been different.' Her voice was hoarse as she finally voiced thoughts that she'd never shared before. 'We were always the careful ones, you and I. He was always the daredevil.'

'He was an adult and he made his own choices.' Finn's fingers tightened on her arms, as if by his grip alone he could pass some of his strength to her. 'You and I being there wouldn't have changed anything, Jules.'

She shook her head and closed her eyes briefly. 'You don't know that. It might have done. I would have been there with him but I was wrapped up in myself and the baby. I wasn't thinking about him.' She swallowed and rubbed her fingers over her forehead. 'I have dreams. He's falling and I can't catch him…'

Finn let out a long breath. 'Guilt is part of grieving,

you know that, sweetheart. But there was nothing you could have done. And there's nothing you can do now.' He paused. 'And it isn't going to bring him back if you die on this mountain.'

She rubbed her eyes and pulled away from him. 'I'm not going to die up here. On the contrary, I want to make it a safer place. I want to be here when people get sick so that I can get them down before they die. I want to stop other families suffering the way mine has.'

Finn let out a long breath. 'You chose to specialise in high-altitude medicine because of Dan and your father, I know that.'

'I've lost two people I love to the mountains,' Juliet said, her voice dull as she wandered to the edge of the tent. 'And it all seems such a pointless waste.' She threw her head back and stared up at the menacing tumble of ice that stood guard over the base of Everest. It had a raw, vicious beauty that caught the breath and stopped the heart. 'And then you come here and you see all this and you understand.'

Finn nodded. 'It's addictive. Pure. Man against nature. Up here life's trivial, problems cease to matter. It's all about survival. Man and the mountain. The ultimate challenge.' He took a deep breath. 'I loved Dan, too, you know that, but that didn't make me blind to the man he was. He was wild and difficult at the best of times. If he didn't want to descend, there was no one on this earth who could have made him do it. Not you or me.'

'I'd rather we didn't talk about it any more. It's over.'

And she wanted to lock the grief away again.

Finn studied her in silence and then he stirred. 'But it's not over,' he said slowly. 'He's the reason you refuse to get involved with anyone. He's the reason you don't have a personal life. So it's far from over.'

Why wouldn't he let the subject drop? Why?

'I have a perfectly satisfactory personal life. I admit I'm pretty nomadic, but climbers usually are. You know that. You're the same.'

'And I think we must be completely crazy.' He ran a hand over the back of his neck and gave a wry smile. 'I used to look at you when you were only eight, climbing like a pro. Just like your damned brother. We were all a bit crazy, weren't we?'

'Try being the child of two explorers. My whole family was crazy,' she muttered, and he gave a humourless laugh.

'Yes, you certainly didn't have the most conventional upbringing.'

'I used to think that traveling across Antarctica and climbing high mountains was what every dad did,' she said lightly. 'So when my brother started climbing the 8000-metre peaks, it just seemed normal. My family spent their whole time challenging nature and risking death. I lost my dad on Annapurna and then I lost Dan on Everest.' She broke off and swallowed hard. 'Let's just say I've seen firsthand how climbing can wreck families. Even those who understand the need to climb.'

There was a long silence and then he finally spoke. 'And that's why you ran out on me, wasn't it? Because you were afraid of love?'

'If I hadn't got pregnant, you never would have asked me to marry you and I wouldn't have said yes,' she said simply. 'There are some people who just shouldn't get married, and I'm one of them. And you're another.'

'That's rubbish.'

'No.' She lifted her head and her eyes sparked. 'It isn't rubbish, Finn. I've lost two people I love in the mountains already and I have to live with that agony every single day. And I've watched my mother live with the same pain. People like us shouldn't fall in love and we shouldn't get married. It's a selfish, deadly pastime and it isn't compatible with family life.'

'And it's that simple?' He looked at her with ill-concealed frustration. 'Love isn't something that you just switch on and off, Jules. You don't decide when to fall in love. It just happens when you meet the right person.'

She felt emotions stir inside her and shut them all down with her usual determination and a stubborn lift of her chin. 'If you don't look for love, you won't find it.'

'You mean if you run hard enough it just might not catch you up.' He looked at her in silence and then shook his head. 'For a brave woman, you're a real coward, do you know that? You'll risk life and limb on Everest but you won't put your heart on the line.'

Something twisted inside her. 'That's my decision.'

'Tell me something, Jules.' Finn's gaze was steady on her face. 'Did you have a horrible childhood?'

She stared for a moment and then she gave a faint smile. 'You know I didn't.'

'Tell me what it was like. How it felt.'

She shrugged. 'Exciting.' She gave a soft smile. 'Amazing. Unconventional.'

'Were you happy? Did you feel loved?'

She looked at him in surprise. 'Of course. We were a very close family.'

'And that's what's important.' His voice was soft. 'You're looking for ways of making life totally safe and predictable. You're looking for guarantees and there aren't any. Your dad could have been a librarian but he still could have died, Jules. He could have been run over. He could have had a heart attack. Life just doesn't come with guarantees, which is all the more reason to live it the way you want to live it. That's what your dad did, and that's what Dan did.'

Her eyes sparkled with unshed tears. 'And what about the people left behind? What about *them?*'

'It's tough. But when you marry a person, you marry all of them. Including their dreams. Climbing is part of who we are but we can minimise the risks. And that's what you're doing here as a doctor, you've already admitted that. It's why you chose high-altitude medicine as your specialty. It's about minimising the risks, isn't it? Spotting problems and educating other people to recognise warning signs. Teaching people not to treat these mountains lightly. It's about doing what you have to do as safely as possible. And then getting on with the rest of your life.'

'I am getting on with my life.'

'I wasn't marrying you because you were pregnant, Jules.' His voice was deep and very male. 'I was marrying you because I was in love with you. And you were in love with me, too.'

She shook her head and lifted a hand defensively. 'Not this again.'

'If you hadn't lost the baby we would have married and we would have been happy. If Dan hadn't have died, I would have come after you and I would have told you how I felt.' His mouth tightened. 'But his death came between us. When I came to find you, you refused to see me.'

'Because I was distraught.' She spread her hands in a silent plea for understanding. 'And seeing you reminded me of Dan. We did everything together. We were a three—'

He looked deep into her eyes. 'And that's why you sent me away? Because it was too painful? Not because you were afraid that the same thing might happen to me? Not because you loved me so much you were protecting yourself from yet another potential loss?'

Her heart bolted into the distance. 'No. No.'

He studied her face for a long moment. 'I loved you, Jules. And you loved me.'

The breath jammed in her throat. 'I didn't feel anything. We were friends, Finn, and we never should have been anything more.'

'Really?' He lifted an eyebrow. 'That's interesting, because it certainly isn't how I remember it. That night we made love…' His voice dropped an octave. 'Tell me you don't think about it every single day.'

She gave a soft gasp and her colour rose. 'Finn—'

'That wasn't friendship, Jules. That was love. Passion.'

She covered her ears with her hands and shook her head. 'It was just sex.'

'You were a virgin. You didn't do "just sex".'

'I was young. My hormones were on fire. That's all it was and I'm sorry if that hurts you but it's the truth.' Her heart was thundering with panic and she turned to walk away from him but he grabbed her arm and pulled her back.

'Stop running.'

She jerked her body away from his. 'We've been honest and talked, which is what you wanted. We've talked about Dan. We've talked about the reason we were getting married. That's it. None of it matters any more.'

His eyes glittered dangerously. 'No?' He reached out and grabbed the front of her thin top, bringing her hard against him. 'You don't think this matters? You think I was going to marry you because I was too much of a gentleman to break it off? Well, let's find out just how polite I really am, shall we?'

Juliet felt the rock-solid muscle of his thighs pressed hard against hers, felt the thundering beat of her own heart against her chest, and then he slid his hands around her cheeks and held her face still for his kiss.

She felt the tension mount between them, felt the chemistry sizzle and crackle to life, and then his mouth came down on hers, hot, demanding and merciless.

There was nothing gentle about the kiss, nothing tentative or seeking. It was a full-blown sensual assault designed to drive logical thought from her brain.

Stunned and taken off guard, Juliet lifted her hands to push him away but instead she found herself pulling him closer, asking wordlessly for more.

And he gave her more.

With a harsh groan he dragged the cap from her head and slid his fingers into her hair, his kiss as savage and wild as their surroundings, as if he realised that this could be the last kiss that either of them ever experienced.

And she kissed him back, caught in the grip of such excitement that she couldn't help but respond. Her heart flew, the blood pumped around her body and she felt light-headed and dizzy.

Using only the skill of his mouth, he took her breath, her resolve and her ability to think clearly.

She felt the rough scrape of masculine stubble against the sensitive flesh of her cheek, felt the erotic slide of his tongue against hers and the seductive caress of his hands as they slid down her back and pulled her firmly against him.

And Juliet was lost.

For her there was no past and no future. No people and no mountain. No tragedy and no loss.

There was only this man and what he did to her.

And then he released her, his breathing harsh and unsteady as he stepped backwards. For a long moment their eyes held and the chemistry continued to sizzle and buzz. And then he gave a faint smile and his hands dropped to his sides.

'That's how much of a gentleman I am, Jules.'

And without giving her time to answer, he walked out of the tent, leaving her to sink to the floor of the tent in a boneless heap, staring after him, shaken and stunned.

CHAPTER SIX

HE SHOULDN'T have kissed her.

Finn lay in the relative privacy of his tent with his eyes firmly closed. But closing his eyes did nothing to relieve the throbbing, nagging ache that burned through his body.

He remembered her face, soft and flushed with passion. He remembered the warmth of her mouth and the tiny little gasps she'd made as he'd kissed her senseless.

He remembered her soft, slender curves pressed against his harder frame and just how hard he'd fought to stop himself from ripping off her combat trousers and taking her hard and fast on the floor of the tent without any regard for their surroundings.

Acknowledging just how close he'd come to losing control, he covered his face with his hand and cursed softly.

He'd spent the best part of ten years trying to put her out of his mind and now he'd blown it.

It was ironic, he reflected without a trace of vanity,

that women threw themselves at him wherever he went, and yet the only woman who had ever really stirred his blood ran in the opposite direction.

They'd been best friends for most of their lives and yet never, not once in the whole of their relationship, had she ever told him that she loved him.

And maybe she didn't. In any case, it was irrelevant, he mused wearily, because she had erected such solid protection round her heart and her feelings that no one had access. And it was time he stopped kidding himself that he could break down those barriers. It was time he stopped dreaming.

Juliet was never going to make herself that vulnerable. If she loved him she was never going to admit it to herself, let alone him.

And maybe she didn't love him.

Maybe she was right. Maybe the sex had been all about youth and hormones.

Maybe he'd imagined the incredible connection between them.

He sat up and gave a humourless laugh as he analysed the situation. Wasn't it men who were supposed to be afraid of commitment? Men who were supposed to be allergic to love?

And that was part of the attraction, he acknowledged. Juliet was totally different to the rest of her sex and always had been. At eight years old, when her friends had been playing with dolls, she'd been out climbing sheer rockfaces with her big brother. While her friends had dreamed of clothes, make-up and boyfriends, she'd dreamed of mountains and snow and untouched horizons.

She was wild and passionate and fearless when it came to testing herself physically, but when it came to relationships…

He stared out of his tent at the harsh, forbidding terrain and let out a long breath. When it came to relationships, Juliet Adams was nothing short of a disaster.

She avoided emotional attachments and ran a mile from commitment, but that was all part of the woman and part of the reason that he had always found her totally irresistible.

He loved her wild, unpredictable nature, her strength and her vulnerability, and he loved a challenge. And Juliet presented the biggest challenge that he was ever likely to find.

He needed to forget her, he told himself firmly, gathering up his water bottles to take them to the mess tent.

Juliet and love didn't go together.

He'd climb this damn mountain and then move on.

The next day they held a *puja,* a traditional Sherpa ceremony to ask the gods for their blessing to climb the mountain. Without this, none of the Sherpas would be prepared to go any further and, in preparation, they'd spent the best part of a day shifting stones to build an altar.

Juliet stood alone at the edge of the circle of people, listening to the chant of the Buddhist priest, the lama, who sat cross-legged on an old mat in the middle of a large rock. Occasionally he broke off to throw flour and rice high into the air as a gift to the gods.

She loved this ceremony and she respected their culture. To them the mountain was sacred and had to give her permission for them to be on her slopes. It would be bad luck to climb without a successful *puja*.

Branches of juniper crackled and burned in the fire and she stood absorbing the scene, her mind totally distracted.

All she could think about was Finn. Their conversation. *And the way he'd kissed her.*

How could she have forgotten how it felt? The heat of his mouth on hers.

Even now, so many hours afterwards, her lips were still tingling and her body was quivering with frustration.

The lama continued to sing and chant prayers until finally he gave the signal and the Sherpas lifted the *puja* prayer pole into position, a long stick of bamboo. Lengths of coloured prayer flags representing the elements—earth, water, fire, cloud and sky—stretched from the top of the pole and were secured to the glacier by heavy rocks. The flags fluttered and spun around in the wind, an eye-catching splash of colour that brightened the drab, glacial terrain and lifted the mood.

Juliet threw rice and flour and took the alcohol handed to her by a grinning Sherpa.

She took a sip, choked and then froze as Finn walked up behind her.

'Drink,' he said in an undertone, 'or you risk offending them and their mountain goddess.'

He looked tough and male and unbelievably sexy,

and she felt her stomach drop. How had she managed to live without him in her life for so long? 'Just as long as you're ready to resuscitate me when I collapse from alcohol poisoning,' she muttered, taking another reluctant sip and trying not to screw her face up. Maybe the alcohol would dull her senses. *Maybe it would make her less aware of Finn.* 'I don't know how they can drink this stuff. It's like paint stripper.'

'They're going to have headaches tomorrow.' Finn smiled down at her and threw another handful of sacred flour into the air. 'I just had a call from the clinic in Pheriche. Your injured Swedish climber is doing well, Dr Adams.'

Did he know how good-looking he was? 'That's good news.'

The temperature suddenly dropped and Juliet huddled deeper into her down jacket.

For her the religious ceremony had great significance because it meant that tomorrow they would climb into the dreaded icefall for the first time.

Juliet glanced over her shoulder towards the daunting, threatening frozen waterfall that guarded this route up the world's highest mountain. *What perils lay ahead?*

'Makes you wonder why we do it, doesn't it?' Finn stood beside her, his gaze following hers, understanding in his dark eyes as he turned to look at her.

'Plenty of people wonder exactly that. I even wonder it myself sometimes.'

Her mother had lost a husband and a son and yet still she was here. The surviving daughter…

Finn nodded, a slight smile touching his hard mouth. 'But we know why, don't we?' His voice was soft and she nodded.

'There isn't anywhere like the mountains.' She tilted her head back and breathed, inhaling the scent of cold air and burning juniper. 'When I'm up there I think about nothing but the next step. Survival.'

Perhaps only another climber truly understood the climber's need to reach the top, to tackle new peaks in the face of extraordinary danger; how the outside world, with all its trivial problems and complications, somehow ceased to exist.

Finn understood. Finn felt the same way. *It was why he'd always been so dangerous.* Apart from her brother, he was the only person who had ever truly understood her.

The atmosphere was becoming more and more merry as the Sherpas consumed increasing quantities of the local brew.

Then the lama offered to bless their climbing equipment and they all went back to their tents to retrieve various bits and pieces.

Juliet brought three different ice axes which she placed on the altar.

Finally the lama left and the various teams wandered back to their tents to make their own preparations for the next day.

The fun and the celebrations were over.

Tomorrow the tone would be serious. They would begin the climb.

* * *

Juliet and the rest of her team rose in darkness to start the climb through the icefall to Camp I. The smell of burning juniper still wafted over Base Camp, an offering to the 'goddess of the sky' from the Sherpas.

At the edge of the icefall Juliet fastened her crampons, the sharp spikes that attached to the boots and enabled a climber to walk on snow and ice.

The cold night air bit through the padding of her clothing and for a moment she thought longingly of her tent and her sleeping bag.

This was undoubtedly the hardest thing about climbing at high altitude, she reflected as she started the walk into the icefall, feeling her crampons bite hard into the ice. During the day the sun's blaze would weaken the ice and walking in such hot temperatures was too exhausting, so much of the climbing was done in darkness.

She clipped the karabiner that was attached to her harness to the fixed rope that ran upwards along the icy terrain. At the beginning of each season a group of skilled Sherpas—the 'icefall doctors'—and climbers established a route through to Camp I using ropes and ladders as a means of crossing the many lethal crevasses that lay deep and deadly, ready to swallow up an unlucky or careless climber.

The route shifted with the movement of the ice and needed to be regularly maintained. Above her, huge blocks of ice hovered in frozen suspension, silent and threatening, each section in danger of imminent collapse.

The truth was that, no matter how many ropes or ladders were used, the Khumbu Icefall would never be safe.

Approaching the first ladder crossing, Juliet paused and wondered for a wild, terrifying moment what she was doing. She was about to walk above a yawning chasm on a ladder, wearing a pair of unwieldy boots with spikes attached.

She knew only too well that the impression of safety was simply an illusion. The icefall was a living, moving thing. A crevasse could shift, sending a ladder tumbling down into fathomless depths. An ice screw could come loose; a rope might not hold. Her crampons might stick on the rungs of the ladder—

'Jules?' Finn trudged up behind her at a steady pace, careful not to expend too much energy. 'Are you OK?'

'I'm fine.' With a determined gesture she placed her foot on the ladder, letting the rung settle between the teeth of her crampons. Then she picked her way carefully across, trying not to look at what lay below. *Trying not to think about falling.*

But she didn't lose her footing and she moved steadily onwards and upwards, clipping onto the next rope, crossing the next ladder, and then the next until she finally stopped for a rest and a drink. She was panting for breath.

The sun was growing stronger and she applied thick sunblock, knowing that skin could burn in a matter of minutes.

Blue ice stretched up above her, as high as an office block, and she saw the surface glistening in the heat of the sun.

Deciding that to rest for too long simply increased the likelihood of disaster, she forced herself to carry on.

An hour later she still wasn't near the top of the ice-fall and Camp I, and Finn trudged up to her.

'It's getting late to be up here. We need to turn around.'

She took several deep breaths, sucking the thin air into her lungs, swamped by disappointment. 'I'm too slow.'

Finn watched her. 'It's your first time in the icefall. You'll be faster next time. You know how it works.'

'Yeah.' She knew how it worked. Each time you climbed slightly higher and the increase in height allowed the body to gradually adjust to the altitude. Theoretically. Not everyone did. She knew plenty of people who never made it out of Base Camp.

'We'll turn around and if you get really lucky I'll buy you a yak burger for supper.' Finn reached out and put a hand on her shoulder and she knew he understood her disappointment.

'I wanted to make it to Camp I today.'

His firm mouth curved into a smile. 'Typical Jules. Always racing ahead. Always aiming high.'

'*I can do it.*'

'I know you can do it.' His hand dropped to his side. 'But not today. Today you're going back down before this place becomes any more dangerous than it already is.'

She didn't argue with him because she knew he was right. It was time to go back down.

She looked at him, noticing how strong he looked and how easy he made it seem, and it occurred to her that he should have been ahead of her. A long way ahead. And yet he was behind her.

'Are you taking on the role of bodyguard?' She glared at him suspiciously and he gave a shrug, not pretending to misunderstand her.

'I'm climbing the way I always climb.'

She narrowed her eyes but decided that this was not the place to pursue the subject. They were standing in lethal terrain and they needed to get away from it.

Finn proved to be right in his prediction.

The next time she climbed through the icefall she was much faster, aided by the fact that her body was gradually acclimatising to the altitude.

Five exhausting hours after she'd left Base Camp, she hauled her body over the lip of a huge serac and saw the Western Cwm, the huge bowl at the top of the icefall. The mountains rose from this plateau and the scenery was breathtaking. This section of the climb was relatively protected from the wind and she knew that temperatures here could soar to more than 30 degrees Celsius and then drop below freezing in a matter of minutes as the sun plunged behind the surrounding mountains. Up here, an unprotected climber could burn severely in minutes.

She lay for a moment, struggling for breath, her eyes on the view.

'Do I need to give you the kiss of life?' Finn slumped down next to her and put a hand on her shoulder. 'Are you all right?'

'I'm more than all right.' Despite her exhaustion and the fact that she could hardly breathe, she grinned at him and then waved an arm. 'Just look at that…'

'I'm looking.'

They sat for a while in silence, their problems temporarily forgotten while they shared the beauty, and then they finally lumbered to their feet and staggered towards the tents.

Camp I, 6100 metres above sea level

They spent the night at Camp I to acclimatise.

Juliet slept fitfully, crammed in the tent that she was sharing with Anna, the only other woman in their party, knowing that this pattern would continue now until they made their summit bid in a few weeks. They would climb up and down the lower sections of the mountain, getting gradually higher to force the body to acclimatise and then dropping down again to allow the body time to recover.

She woke early in the morning when Anna sat up and a shower of icicles fell from the inside of the tent onto her sleeping bag.

'Ugh. Thanks a lot.' Juliet sat up, groggy and breathless and coughing badly. 'Talk about starting the day with a cold shower.'

Anna gave a shudder. 'You forget how much colder it is up here,' she muttered as she finished dressing and shuffled towards the entrance of the tent. 'Your cough sounds bad. And you're our doctor.'

'Everyone coughs up here,' Juliet croaked, dressing as quickly as she could and pulling her hood up tight. Outside the tent the wind would be biting cold and she wanted to be as well prepared as possible. Her head was pounding and she felt dehydrated, despite all the water she was trying to drink.

Today they were planning to climb a little higher towards Camp II before dropping back to Base Camp for a rest.

She wondered, not for the first time, how she was ever going to get any higher than this and yet, before the climb was over, she would have climbed back up through the icefall and Camp I more times than she wanted to count.

Best not to think about it, she decided as she fastened her crampons before pushing the rest of her equipment back into her rucksack and unzipping the door of the tent.

Best just to concentrate on today.

Finn was climbing with them and from time to time Juliet stopped to rest and watch him in action.

His movements were skilled and economical, designed to conserve energy and minimise risk. He was strong and sure and steady, totally at home in these harsh surroundings.

And he was nothing like her brother.

Even as a child she'd been aware of the differences between them. Her brother had embraced risk, even courted it in a wild, almost adolescent carelessness for the fragility of life. In contrast, Finn was mature and careful in his decision-making, skilled and steady, measuring and minimising risk wherever possible.

Juliet trudged across the Western Cwm, painfully slowly, aware only of her own breathing and the heat of the sun in the airless, scorching desert of snow and ice.

She'd stopped to rest when Billy and Finn came back along the rope towards her.

'They've had a problem in the icefall. One of the Sherpas has fallen into a crevasse near the top.'

'Again?' Juliet sucked in the oxygen-depleted air and tried to clear the muzzy feeling in her brain.

'The icefall is particularly dangerous this year,' Billy agreed, watching as she clipped herself onto the next section of fixed rope.

She was only a short distance up the slope to Camp II. She could be back down to Camp I at the top of the icefall in less than twenty minutes.

'Let's go.' Without arguing or wasting precious time asking questions that Billy wouldn't be able to answer, she turned and started to plod back down, grateful for the thick layer of sun cream and her sunglasses.

She was slower than the others and when she eventually reached the top of the icefall she saw several figures bunched together over a body lying on the snow.

She plodded up to them and then stood for a moment, gasping for breath and coughing hard. 'What's the damage?'

'We're just taking his suit off to take a better look.' Finn frowned at her. 'You walked too fast. How long have you had that cough?'

'It's nothing. I'm fine. Everyone coughs up here, you know that as well as I do.' She took her pack off her back and then dropped to her knees beside the injured climber, recognising him immediately as one of the Sherpas leading the New Zealand team. 'Lopsang.'

The Sherpa gave her a weak smile but it was obvious that he was in a great deal of pain and once his down suit had been removed it was possible to see why.

'I felt it break when I landed and crunching when I tried to move. Very bad damage,' he groaned, and Juliet exchanged looks with Finn.

Both of them suspected that they were dealing with a lower leg fracture and an injury of that severity above the treacherous icefall was no joke. Evacuating him was going to be problematic, to say the least.

'There's swelling and bruising over the tibia,' Juliet muttered, gently palpating the injured leg and comparing it to the uninjured leg, 'and it's obviously very tender. Did he fall far?'

One of the other climbers, who had been just behind Lopsang, recounted what had happened while Juliet continued examining the injured man.

'There's spasm of the surrounding muscles and it feels very rigid.' She checked the circulation distal to the suspected fracture and then glanced at Finn, who was spreading out equipment. 'His pulses are OK at the moment but we need to splint it and get him down somehow.'

'I agree. We'll splint a joint above and below the injury using ice axes and we'll use sleeping pads for comfort,' Finn said calmly. 'And we need to keep a close eye on his distal circulation and before and after splinting.'

They worked smoothly together to apply the splint and once it was in place they checked the Sherpa's circulation again.

'Can you feel this?' Finn checked for sensation and movement and then gave a satisfied nod. 'That's fine at the moment but we need to keep checking to make sure that the splint wrap isn't too tight. We'll recheck pulses, capillary refill and distal limb colour periodically, along with nerve function. Lopsang, any change in sensation or pain, I want you to tell us. Loudly. Understood?'

The Sherpa gave a weak nod. 'Understood, Dr Finn.'

While they'd been stabilising the injured Sherpa the other climbers had been planning the evacuation. Transporting an injured climber from the icefall down to Base Camp was a risky business that required much thought, effort and co-operation on everyone's part.

'He can't walk. We could ask for a helicopter evacuation,' Juliet suggested tentatively, but Finn shook his head.

'It's been done, of course.' He gave a rueful smile. 'The highest Himalayan rescue in history. But we have to remember that you're risking the life of the pilot. If we can get this chap down by stretcher, that's what we'll do.'

Juliet sat back and nodded agreement, knowing that he was right. And his measured, thoughtful approach was just another example of the way Finn handled risk.

He wasn't prepared to endanger the pilot's life by requesting an evacuation from Camp I if it was possible to get the injured climber down any other way.

'There's plenty of us up here at the moment.' Finn glanced at the number of climbers milling around. 'We can get him down.'

And they did.

With the help of amazing teamwork from Sherpas and climbers from all countries, they finally trudged into Base Camp four hours later.

Finn and Juliet took the injured climber back to the Everest expedition medical tent while the others set about shifting rocks and flattening a large enough area of Base Camp for a helicopter landing.

'We need to make sure there's no loose dirt or snow. The helicopters are modified but, even so, flying at 17,600 feet is a dangerous enough undertaking without the additional hazards of flying debris. He'll come in the early morning, while the air pressure is at its highest,' Finn said, removing the bandages from the climber's leg and checking the circulation. 'Let's hope for good weather.'

There was a sprinkling of snow over Base Camp but the skies were clear and early next morning they heard the familiar *clack-clack-clack* of the approaching helicopter.

Finn had cleared the area and ensured that all tents

and loose objects had been secured and that everyone knew the drill.

Juliet was preparing to move her injured patient out of the medical tent when the noise of the helicopter abruptly ceased.

For a few breathless seconds she stood still, her hand on Lopsang's splinted leg, trying to work out why it had gone quiet.

And then Finn muttered, 'Oh, my God.' She heard a hideous grinding, crashing noise as the helicopter plummeted onto the rocky surface of Base Camp.

'He's lost control.' Finn was out of the tent in an instant, immediately assessing the damage and taking charge. In his usual calm, authoritative way he kept people back from the helicopter, gesturing to Juliet to follow him. 'We need to get them out.'

She followed him, scrambling over boulders and rubble, slipping on patches of snow, her heart thudding hard from exertion and reaction.

The helicopter lay on its side like a huge, felled beast and as they reached it the door opened and the pilot scrambled out, blood pouring from a wound on his head, his eyes shocked.

'Take him to the tent and get some oxygen straight on him,' Finn ordered grimly, and Juliet nodded, knowing that the pilot had come straight up from the Kathmandu valley and used oxygen to make the flight to this altitude. Without additional oxygen now he would soon develop AMS—acute mountain sickness.

He ran the risk of becoming severely ill very quickly.

It was a reminder to all of them just how high they really were, she thought as she introduced herself to the pilot and slipped an arm round him to give him some support.

Billy stepped forward to help her and together they left Finn to deal with the copilot while they helped the pilot to the medical tent.

Juliet gave him oxygen and then examined him swiftly. The cut on his head was superficial and she cleaned and dressed it and then looked up as Finn arrived with the copilot.

He, too, appeared relatively uninjured, which was nothing short of a miracle.

'They're heroes, even attempting to fly up here,' Finn muttered as he handed the copilot an oxygen mask and gave him a thorough examination. 'I can't believe their injuries aren't worse.'

'I've radioed for another helicopter,' Billy said, coming back into the tent to reassess the situation. 'They can take Lopsang and then come back for the pilot and copilot. We're going to sort out a suitable landing spot.'

Juliet glanced up as a Sherpa appeared in the doorway, looking apologetic. He was complaining of a terrible headache and she gave him some aspirin just as Neil appeared.

'Looks like I've been missing all the action.' He grinned and glanced back at the downed helicopter with a shake of his head. 'Can't you get anything right without me?'

Juliet smiled, pleased to see him. 'Drama, drama, drama,' she said wearily. 'Just don't you collapse on me or I'll fire you from the team. How's your headache?'

'Gone. I'm fully acclimatised. Fit as a fiddle.' Neil flexed his muscles. 'And just to prove it, I'll go and heave boulders with Billy.'

The second helicopter made two journeys to evacuate the Sherpa and the pilots of the abandoned aircraft and two hours later everything at Base Camp was once more quiet.

That evening the Everest expedition team joined Finn's team for 'dinner', which turned out to be yak stew and rice.

'I'm definitely turning vegetarian,' Juliet muttered, nibbling the meat cautiously and then wishing she hadn't. 'I think I'll stick to the rice.'

'You'll never grow big and strong like that.' Neil reached across and helped himself to her meat. 'Won't reach the top of Everest if you don't eat.'

Juliet caught Finn looking at her and knew what he was thinking.

That she shouldn't be going to the top of Everest at all.

After dinner they all gathered in the mess tent to watch a DVD and Juliet marvelled on how incongruous it was, to be sitting where they were, watching a film.

Somehow she found herself seated next to Finn and she could feel the hard press of his thigh against hers and the brush of his shoulder.

Her whole body tingled with awareness.

He was the only man who had ever done this to her.

The only man to make her feel like a complete woman, no matter what the circumstances.

Here they were, at a ridiculously high altitude, wearing thick clothing, and all she could think about was what it would be like to kiss him again.

She cursed herself mentally and tried to concentrate on the film.

She'd rebuilt her life without him and now, seeing him and working so closely with him, had somehow unravelled her.

She was feeling things that she didn't want to feel. *Things that she hadn't felt for years.*

It was just attraction, she told herself firmly. Finn was a staggeringly attractive man and if she was in any doubt about that, she only had to watch the way all the other females in Base Camp gravitated towards him, hoping to snare his interest.

Even now, Anna, from her own team, was smiling at him flirtatiously from across the room as they argued a point about climbing technique.

Juliet felt something twist inside her.

She wasn't jealous. She absolutely wasn't. Because to admit that she was jealous would mean admitting that she had feelings for Finn. And she didn't. She absolutely didn't.

He was a friend, nothing more.

And she needed to keep her distance from him.

CHAPTER SEVEN

OVER the next week the various teams climbed up to the different camps in their preparations for the push to the summit, which would hopefully come in early May.

Juliet spent a grim, freezing night at Camp II before descending back to Base Camp where she found herself kept busy seeing a steady stream of sick climbers and Sherpas.

Finn was up on the mountain, and when he finally descended she managed to keep herself so busy that they barely saw each other for almost a week.

Not all the expeditions had doctors with them and she was more than happy to help anyone she could, relieved that she'd been generous when she'd been judging the quantities of supplies to bring on the trip.

A nasty stomach virus attacked Base Camp and laid everyone low for several days, followed by a fever and cough which managed to keep a large proportion of the teams off the mountain for several days.

The weather gradually deteriorated and Base Camp

was battered by howling winds that threatened to drag the tents from the snow-covered glacier and hurl them down into the valley.

Wondering what it must be like for the climbers high up on the mountain in the current storm, Juliet lay huddled in her tent, wearing almost all the clothes she possessed, listening to the screaming howl of the wind and wondering whether the tent was going to blow away, taking her with it.

Through the shrieking of the wind she heard her name and struggled forward to unzip her tent, wondering who on earth needed her in these conditions.

Finn pushed through the flap, bringing a flurry of snow and freezing air with him. He turned and zipped the tent up behind him with a gloved hand. 'I was just checking up on you.' His powerful shoulders dominated the confined space and Juliet wriggled back against the tent wall and immediately regretted it as snow showered over her.

She shivered. 'You let all the cold into my nice warm house,' she muttered sarcastically, and he grinned.

'You always did have a penchant for five-star accommodation.' He glanced around him and then back at her. 'Only on Everest does it snow inside your tent. Are you all right?'

Her teeth were chattering. 'Why wouldn't I be?'

'Well, for a start you rejected your yak for supper yet again,' he said in a conversational tone, 'which means that you're considerably lighter than the rest of us. I'd hate you to be blown away down the valley.'

'Is that why you're here?' She huddled deeper into her down jacket. 'To help weigh my tent down?'

'Something like that.' His gaze roamed over her face. 'I've hardly seen you the last week. You've turned into the unofficial Base Camp doctor. All I hear is praise for Dr Juliet.'

She tried to smile but her teeth were chattering too much. 'I'm glad I'm down here and not up there.'

He nodded. 'Camp IV is being hammered by winds. These are prime conditions for developing frostbite. If the weather doesn't improve, no one will be going for the summit for a while. The forecast is terrible.' He reached out a hand and touched her face. 'You're losing weight, Jules.'

'Everyone loses weight at this altitude,' she croaked, trying not to react to his touch. 'It's basic physiology. You know that as well as I do. Up here the body gradually deteriorates.'

Finn gave a crooked smile. 'Your body still looks fine to me. Or I should say, what I can see of it underneath that sexy gear you're wearing looks fine to me.'

Despite the cold, she couldn't help laughing. *He'd always been able to make her laugh.* Her heart bumped against her chest. 'How long do you think this storm will last?'

He shrugged. 'Who knows? It's not looking good though. Why?' His eyes narrowed. 'Are you scared?'

She glared at him, her green eyes fierce. 'I'm not scared of anything.'

He gave a soft laugh. 'Oh, yes, you are, sweetheart.'

His gaze dropped to her mouth and lingered there. 'You're afraid of standing in front of an altar and say-ing "I do". You're afraid of commitment. You're afraid of loving and you're afraid of losing.'

The wind screamed around the tent, obliterating all other sounds, giving them total privacy. The other climbers might as well have been a million miles away.

Trapped in the confined space of the tent, she was breathlessly aware of every male inch of him. 'I'm sorry about everything, Finn. I just want you to know that.' *Who knew what might happen in the next few days up on Everest's slopes?* There were things that she needed to say and she knew she had to say them now. 'I didn't think about you. Just about me.'

'You were confused, scared and sad about the baby,' he said roughly, letting his hand fall to his side. 'I under-stood.'

'I know it was an accident but I wanted our baby,' she whispered, and he nodded.

'I know you did. I wanted it, too. We should have talked about it at the time.'

She shook her head. 'I just couldn't. It was weird. Part of me was terrified by the responsibility but an-other part of me was thrilled to be pregnant. Then I lost it and it was like a sign…'

Finn let out a long breath. 'It wasn't a sign, Jules. It was just nature being her cruel self, sweetheart.'

She wrapped her arms round her waist. 'If I hadn't lost the baby—'

'We'd be happily married.'

'I'd be at home with our child and you'd be up here, risking your life,' she said flatly, and he looked at her in silence for a long time.

'Is that what you think?'

'I've seen it over and over again, and so have you.' She ignored the sudden shriek of the wind that almost drowned their conversation and she ignored the increasing chill of her fingers and toes. 'Climbing mountains is not compatible with family life.'

'There are plenty of climbers who have perfectly rewarding family lives.'

'It would never have worked.'

He slid a hand behind her head and forced her to look at him. 'Tell me you loved me, Jules.'

She stared at him, her heart thundering against her chest. 'I didn't love you.'

She'd never been in love. She'd seen the agony of love firsthand and she'd always promised herself that it wasn't going to happen to her. She made sure it didn't.

Frustration, irritation and something approaching anger flickered in his dark eyes. 'Jules—'

'I'm sorry, Finn,' she croaked, jerking her head away from his hand, 'but I don't love you. We would have got married because of the baby. That's all true. But I don't love you and I never did.'

He stared at her for a long moment, his eyes hard and his jaw tense.

And then he moved back to the entrance of her tent and dragged down the zip.

Juliet watched him go, her thoughts numb and tangled.

She didn't love him. She didn't. She just didn't.

So why, since he'd left, did the air suddenly seem so much colder?

And why did her tent seem bleaker and more lonely?

Her feelings clearly didn't go beyond friendship.

Finn lay in the privacy of his own tent, listening to the relentless assault of the wind and the deep, agonising groans of the glacier beneath him. It was almost as if the mountain was exploding in a fit of temper, reflecting his own anger.

Because he *was* angry.

With Juliet. With life for dealing them a lousy hand. *But mostly with himself.*

He'd been so sure that she loved him. *So sure…*

And yet he was starting to believe that he'd made a serious misjudgment.

He'd thought she was afraid of commitment. He'd believed she was afraid to allow herself to love.

But he'd never, once, no matter what the circumstances, been able to persuade her to admit that she loved him. So maybe she didn't. Maybe she never had.

Perhaps he was being arrogant in even thinking that she had.

Now it was time to give up.

Time to move on and acknowledge that Juliet Adams didn't have feelings for him and never would.

He was going to climb this mountain and then put thoughts and memories of her well and truly behind him.

He was going to get on with his life.

The storm had eased by dawn and Juliet gingerly opened the zip on her tent and surveyed the damage to Base Camp.

Several tents had been ripped by the wind but things could have been worse.

'Dr Juliet.' The Sherpa who did the cooking for their expedition brought her a cup of hot tea which she accepted with a grateful smile.

Her head was throbbing, her chest was hurting and she felt run-down and exhausted.

She still wasn't sleeping well but suddenly her dreams were all about Finn. Finn kissing her. Finn stripping off her clothes…

With an impatient sound she concentrated on her tea and told herself firmly that anything was better than nightmares about her brother.

She took an aspirin, hoping that it would relieve her headache, and resolved to drink as much liquid as she possibly could over the coming day.

Suddenly she thought of Simon and his comment that climbing Everest was 'easy'. She wished he were here now, with his feet in her boots, experiencing what she was.

There was certainly nothing easy about it, she thought gloomily as she forced herself to pull on extra layers and walk over to the mess tent for breakfast.

The altitude had totally killed her appetite but she knew the importance of eating so she tried to force down some mouthfuls of porridge, even though the effort nearly choked her and she felt physically sick.

Around the camp climbers were emerging from tents, assessing and repairing any damage caused by the high winds, exchanging information on the higher camps.

'The Russians have lost two tents at Camp III,' Billy told Juliet as he joined her in the mess tent, 'and the winds will delay laying ropes up to Camp IV. But on the whole we're doing all right. Tomorrow you can push on up to Camp III.'

Juliet gave up on food and forced herself to drink. She couldn't imagine having the energy to climb up to Camp III but she knew that somehow she'd manage it.

Resolving to have as quiet a day as possible, she spent the time checking her equipment, making sure that everything was in good order for the climb ahead.

Several times during the day she spotted Finn, but he merely nodded in her direction and spent the time with his own team.

And she wasn't missing him, she told herself firmly as she laid out her crampons and selected two ice axes. They were friends, nothing more. Colleagues. She wasn't disappointed that he hadn't come over to talk to her. Not at all. In fact, she was relieved, because she didn't want the entire camp speculating on the exact nature of their relationship.

Fortunately the weather had been too wild for anyone to have noticed his presence in her tent the previous night.

Juliet tried to occupy herself but inside she felt heavy and flat and couldn't work out why.

Usually she loved being in the mountains but today the snowy flanks of Everest seemed threatening and menacing and the creaks and groans of the icefall seemed to be a warning not to enter.

And in two days she'd be back up there.

Risking her neck to climb a mountain that had already claimed the life of her brother.

Was Finn right?

Was she doing it for the wrong reasons?

If it weren't for Dan, would she be here?

'Dr Juliet, come quickly!'

Juliet woke from a light sleep to find one of the Sherpas hovering by the entrance to her tent, shining a flashlight directly in her eyes.

She sat up and put a hand over her eyes, still groggy, crushed by the lack of air and the nagging, throbbing pain in her head that never seemed to ease. 'What's happened?'

'A climber is very sick, Dr Juliet. You must come quickly. Dr Finn says it is urgent.' The flashlight was still shining in her face and she squinted as she struggled out of her sleeping bag, gasping as the cold night air bit straight through to her bones.

'Sick?' Shivering and tired, she dragged on her down jacket, moving as quickly as she could. 'Who is sick?'

'Spanish boy very sick.'

Juliet frowned. The Spaniards were a small, experienced team who were travelling without a doctor. She knew that they'd already been up as far as Camp III and had seemed to be doing well.

She walked the short distance to their tents and found Finn already on his knees, examining the sick climber who was writhing and moaning on the floor and coughing up blood-stained, frothy sputum.

For a moment Juliet froze.

She knew exactly what she was seeing.

As she watched, Finn pushed his knuckles hard into the man's sternum and the climber waved an arm to push him away.

'He's responding to painful stimulae.' Finn glanced up at her, a stethoscope looped round his neck and a grim expression on his handsome face, 'but nothing else. His pulse and respirations are rapid and I'm hearing crackles in his chest. To be honest, I don't even need to use the stethoscope. It sounds like sucking liquid through a straw.'

Juliet dropped to her knees beside him, noticing that the man's skin was clammy and pale.

'He's showing all the signs of HAPE.' High-altitude pulmonary oedema was a potentially fatal illness in which the lungs filled with fluid. Invariably it was brought on by climbing too high, too fast, and the only real cure was a rapid descent. 'Can we get him to the medical tent?'

'Only if we carry him, and I'd rather not lay him flat. Better to bring everything to him if we can.'

Several climbers and Sherpas hovered expectantly in the entrance of the tent, waiting for them to do something and share the responsibility.

Suddenly she was glad that Finn was here, too. The knowledge that she wasn't alone in this situation helped her think more clearly.

'What do you want us to do?' Billy stood calmly in the entrance of the tent, awaiting instructions, and Finn didn't hesitate.

'What we really need to do is get him down to a lower altitude, but given that we can't do that until tomorrow morning at the earliest I need dexamathasone, nifedipine and oxygen to start with.' Finn gave instructions as to where they could all be found and Billy listened carefully.

'Do you want to use the gammow bag?'

The gammow bag was a double-skinned, inflatable plastic chamber which, when pressurised, had the effect of lowering the apparent altitude by several thousand metres.

'At the moment I don't want to risk laying him flat,' Finn said calmly, 'but some more layers would be useful. The cold raises pulmonary artery pressure and we're in enough trouble here as it is.'

Billy went off to do as requested, without wasting time asking further questions, and Juliet reflected on just how good teamwork was on the mountain. Although everyone had their individual goals, no one hesitated to put aside their own dreams when someone else was in need of assistance.

Someone brought a propane heater into the tent and covered Carlos with several sleeping bags. Juliet continued to check his oxygen saturation.

'It's thirty-four.' She looked at Finn, trying not to let her expression show her anxiety. The level of oxygen in Carlos's blood was dangerously low, even given the high altitude. As a Sherpa arrived with an oxygen cylinder, she took it from him and slipped the mask over Carlos's face then checked the reading again. 'His sats have gone up to sixty-five already.'

She struggled to stop Carlos from removing the mask and Finn nodded.

'That's good. We'll give him a dose of dex. straight into the muscle and then I'll try and get a line in. All the IV fluid is frozen so there's no point in waiting for that. Someone needs to go and start defrosting it.' He looked up as Billy lumbered into the tent, holding boxes of drugs. 'Any luck?'

Billy nodded. 'I found all of it, I think. You'd better double-check the boxes.'

Juliet grabbed them from him. 'I'll give him the dex.' She agreed with Finn's decision to give dexamethasone—a steroid would help draw fluid out of the tissues and relieve symptoms. She ripped open the syringe and gave one of the boxes back to Billy. 'Open that, will you? He needs to have 10 milligrams of sublingual nifedipine straight away. Push it under his tongue.' She was talking as she worked, preparing to give Carlos an injection which would hopefully help save his life.

Finn glanced up. 'We'll give him another 20 milligrams of slow-release four times a day until we get him out of here, and also acetazolomide.'

Juliet gave the injection quickly, hoping that it would have some effect. 'We need to get him down to Kathmandu.'

'Then let's hope for good weather tomorrow,' Finn said, his gaze concentrated on the sick climber's arm. He found a vein, sited an IV and taped it firmly in place. 'Has anyone defrosted any fluid for me yet?'

'It's in the kitchen tent, being defrosted over the gas as we speak.' Billy was hovering, prepared to be a runner for anything and everything they needed. 'Jack's been talking to the rescue guys. They're going to try and land a helicopter here at dawn tomorrow. So let's pray for good weather. One helicopter crash in a season is more than enough.'

Juliet looked at the patient. They were more than seventeen thousand feet above sea level and darkness was falling. There was no chance of a helicopter evacuation until early morning, which meant that Carlos had a long night ahead of him. *And so did they.*

If they couldn't stabilise him, they were going to be in trouble.

Finn looked at her. 'We need to keep an eye on his blood pressure after that nifedipine.'

She nodded, knowing that the drug could lower the blood pressure to a dangerously low level, and at the same time she marvelled at how calm Finn appeared to be. Although she was careful not to display any evidence of tension, inside she didn't feel calm at all.

She'd worked in accident and emergency departments all over the country in England, but all that experience counted for nothing up here. Up here in this frozen, barren, airless wasteland there was no fancy machinery to call on, no second opinions. There was just her and Finn.

And it was medicine in the raw, a true test of a doctor's skills. Up here, her knowledge truly made a difference. Ever since the effects of altitude on human physiology had been recognised, doctors had been trying to find ways of spotting those at risk and reducing fatalities.

It was all about avoiding needless deaths.

Like her brother's.

Is this what had happened to him?

High up in the Death Zone, had he succumbed to pulmonary or cerebral oedema with no one to help get him down?

Dark thoughts bubbled up inside her and for a moment she stilled, her mind distracted.

'We might end up using the gammow bag if he doesn't improve soon,' Finn muttered, and then broke off, a frown on his face as he looked at her. 'Juliet?'

Juliet didn't hear him. She was still locked in a frightening, terrifying world of swirling dark memories.

'Jules!' This time Finn's voice was sharp and penetrated her mental fog.

'Sorry?' She gave a jump. What had she missed? 'Did you say something?'

Finn's eyes were sharp on her face. 'I was saying that I don't want to use the gammow bag now because I want to keep him upright. What do you think?'

Juliet swallowed. 'I—I agree,' she said, her voice slightly croaky. 'His condition is more stable now and his sats have improved. If he gets worse or if the helicopter can't land in the morning, maybe we'll review the situation. I think we should try Salmeterol. I know it's an asthma medication but it also can hasten the body's ability to re-absorb oedema fluid that clogs up the airways in HAPE.'

'Right. Let's do it.' Finn's eyes didn't leave her face. 'Are you all right?'

Conscious that they had an audience of climbers and Sherpas, she gave a brisk nod. 'Fine. Absolutely fine.'

He hesitated and then gave a sigh. 'Liar. But this isn't the time or place, as we both know.'

He saw too much.

He knew everything about her, and always had.

As a child she'd loved the fact that he'd always seemed to know what she'd been thinking and feeling.

Billy stepped forward, shining the torch in their direction so that they could see everything they needed to see in the dark confines of the tent. 'Do you guys want anything else?'

Finn gave a wry smile. 'A decent meal and a warm bed wouldn't go amiss, but I don't suppose that's on offer.'

Billy gave an apologetic smile. 'The honeymoon suite is all booked out but we do have some incredible rooms with mountain views. Any takers?'

'Not tonight,' Juliet said quietly as she checked Carlos's blood pressure and sats again. 'We won't be going anywhere until that helicopter arrives.'

Finn stifled a yawn. 'It's going to be a long night.'

CHAPTER EIGHT

THE helicopter arrived before dawn, making the most of the higher air pressure to gain maximum lift for the rotors.

In order to be able to fly at that altitude, the pilot had stripped the helicopter down to make it as light as possible but still only had enough fuel to stay on the ground for three minutes.

Every time a helicopter landed there was a risk. This time there was no crash. No drama. No disaster.

He landed on the new 'landing pad' that had been hacked out of the rough terrain by a team of Sherpas and climbers.

The deadly whip of the long blades caused a storm of snow and ice and the sound echoed around the valley.

Carlos had been strapped onto a stretcher, sitting upright to aid his breathing, and the climbers loaded him into the helicopter, guided by Finn who was talking to the pilot via a radio.

As soon as the patient was loaded the pilot took off

and the lumbering aircraft swooped down the valley and out of sight.

Finn breathed out heavily and glanced at Juliet. 'Good job.' His voice was soft and she blushed at the praise.

'You, too. We're a good team.'

He looked at her for a long moment and the atmosphere tensed and throbbed around them. Then he gave a brief nod and strolled back across Base Camp towards his tent.

Juliet swallowed.

Colleagues. That's what they were now.

And wasn't that exactly what she'd wanted?

CAMP III, 7300 metres above sea level

They sat together, four of them cramped in a tiny tent that was balanced on a platform hacked from the ice, trying to melt enough ice for drinking. At first the stove had refused to light but eventually it had yielded to their attempts and now it hissed gently.

Above them lay Camp IV on the South Col, a bleak lonely place, deep in the Death Zone where no living thing could survive for long. And above that the summit of Everest.

Their dream.

But they were still a long way from that, Juliet thought wearily as she ripped open a packet of dried food and emptied it into a cup. She wondered why she was bothering. She had no confidence that she'd be able to eat it.

She was tired and she had no appetite, all consequences of the high altitude. Several of her team were talking about dropping further down the valley to the villages before making the final push for the summit, working on the assumption that breathing in the oxygen-rich air lower down would be beneficial to their acclimatisation programme.

Juliet was sorely tempted by the prospect of being able to breathe properly, but, at the same time, was slightly concerned about the strong possibility of contracting a stomach bug, which was always a risk in the Sherpa villages.

Would descending to a lower altitude make her stronger? Give her more energy?

Billy had said that they needed to make the distance between Camp II and Camp III in seven hours if they had a hope of making the summit.

She'd taken closer to eight and Neil had finally slumped into the tent ten hours after leaving Camp II.

He lay now, exhausted and spent, with his eyes closed and Juliet sensed that he had nothing left to give.

They were too slow. She knew they were both too slow.

An avalanche of ice and rocks had ripped tents from the camp, leaving only a few standing. Consequently the expeditions currently on the mountain were sharing while Sherpas brought up more supplies from Base Camp.

Only a climber would understand how totally unromantic it was to be sharing a tent with three bulky men at 24,500 feet, Juliet thought with wry humour.

Billy and Neil were in the tent with her, along with Finn.

The rest of his team had turned back to Camp II after finding the going too tough, and Anna had gone down with them.

Should she have turned back, too? She certainly didn't feel good. Her cough was worse and she felt as though she'd stretched herself to the very limit.

Finn had made the climb in six hours and now sat with his eyes closed in the corner of the tent, recovering.

Juliet longed to wriggle over to him and rest her head on his chest just for a moment. She needed his strength.

Maybe he felt it, too, because his eyes opened and he looked at her for a long moment, his gaze curiously intense.

He'd loved her.

The thought flew into her head and she swallowed hard. *Once, this amazing man had loved her.*

And she'd run away from that love.

She'd chosen to live her life without it. *Without him.*

Suddenly her thoughts twisted and tangled and she felt panicky and confused. It was just the altitude, she told herself firmly. Just this place. It made one long for human comfort.

She reminded herself firmly that she and Finn were colleagues and friends. Nothing more. She wasn't capable of feeling what he claimed to have felt so it had been right not to marry him. She didn't want to feel anything for him. *Didn't dare.*

Finn's eyes held hers and she had a sudden, desperate need to know what he was thinking.

But with two other people squashed in the tiny tent, there was no chance of finding out.

It was Neil who broke the contact between them. From being almost comatose, he suddenly stirred, sat up and wriggled his way to the edge of the tent.

Juliet caught his arm. 'Neil? What are you doing? Where are you going?'

This wasn't a place to go for stroll and enjoy the view. One false step and you were dead.

For a moment he stared at her blankly, as if he didn't recognise her. There was no sign of his usual joviality. 'To the toilet.'

He didn't seem himself and Juliet frowned, her hand still firmly on his arm. 'Crampons, Neil,' she said urgently. 'You haven't put your crampons on.'

Below them was the infamous Lohtse face, five thousand feet of sheer blue ice, ready to tempt the careless climber to his death.

They all knew the rules. No one left the tent without the crampons that would give them a grip on the ice. People had died from making that very mistake.

Neil stared at his feet, as though he hadn't realised they were his responsibility.

'I'll be careful.' He was slurring his words and he stood up and staggered.

Juliet looked at Finn in consternation.

His eyes were sharp now, watchful as he studied Neil, and she knew exactly what he was thinking because she was thinking the same thing.

HACE.

High-altitude cerebral oedema, a severe form of acute mountain sickness in which the brain swelled and ceased to function properly. Loss of co-ordination and an inability to think straight were both possible signs of HACE.

And Juliet knew just how urgent the situation was.

If Neil had cerebral oedema, they had to get him down. Fast.

Even as she was trying to think her way through the next course of action, Neil dropped to his knees and vomited weakly outside the tent.

Finn picked up the radio and Juliet heard him talking to the team at Base Camp, discussing who was already on the mountain and who could come up from the lower camps to help.

She glanced across at him. 'It's pitch dark.' And the deadly ice face lay between them and the lower camps. If they left now, they could die.

But if they stayed…

Finn was still holding the radio. 'You know the treatment as well as I do, Jules.' His voice was rough and his eyes were on Neil, who was still retching outside the tent. 'We have to get him to a lower altitude. And we have to do it fast.'

She knew what he was saying. If they spent the night up here, Neil would be dead in the morning.

'He's too exhausted to walk.'

Finn was already trying to gather his equipment. 'I'll rope him to me. Ken and Alan are climbing up from Camp I. They'll meet us. Billy?'

Billy nodded, his expression worried. 'No problem.'

But Juliet knew it was a big problem. They were all exhausted from the long climb up to Camp III. It had taken nearly everything out of them. To descend in darkness over a treacherous ice face was asking a lot.

Billy looked at Finn. 'She'll have to come, too.'

Finn nodded, his expression grim. 'I know that.' He looked at Juliet and something flickered in his dark gaze. 'She can do it.'

Juliet was touched by his faith in her but had a sinking feeling of dread deep in her stomach. Could she do it? She'd climbed for eight hours. She was exhausted. Drained. The thought of going out in the freezing darkness and making her way down the nearly vertical equivalent of a skating rink didn't hold any appeal. Finn was still watching her and she gave a wan smile. 'No problem.'

Having made the decision to descend, they turned their attention to Neil who was becoming irritable and belligerent, all signs of HACE.

'We'll give him 8 milligrams of dexamethasone immediately and 4 milligrams in another six hours,' Finn said. 'And start him on oxygen.'

'I'm all right,' Neil mumbled, but Juliet was already reaching for one of the small cylinders that were stashed at Camp III. Above this height everyone in her team would be using oxygen and the Sherpas had already left a supply in the tents.

Finn took the mask and tried to fit it to Neil's face.

Immediately he knocked it aside with his hand, a fierce look in his eyes. 'Are you trying to suffocate me?'

Juliet put a hand on Finn's arm. 'Let me,' she said quietly, and she moved forward so that she was next to Neil. 'Look at me, Neil. It's me, Juliet. Stubborn doctor who's afraid of flying. Remember me?'

He stared at her blankly and then something flickered in the depths of his gaze. 'You won't marry me.'

'That's right.' She grinned, ignoring Finn's astonished look. 'I'm not planning on marrying anyone, but do you know what?' She took the mask from Finn. 'If you put this mask on your face and get yourself safely down this mountain, I'll seriously consider it. You just might get lucky.'

Neil swayed slightly and took the mask. His hand was shaking. He put it over his mouth and nose and immediately dropped it. 'It's suffocating me.'

'You just need to give yourself a moment to get used to it,' Juliet urged, her tone soothing, her eyes kind and reassuring. 'You're sick, Neil. You've got cerebral oedema and we need to get you off this mountain.'

He hesitated and then took the mask again and covered his mouth and nose.

Juliet found that she was holding her own breath. She knew how much he needed the oxygen. His brain was gradually deteriorating. If he got any worse they wouldn't be able to get him down, and up here there was no rescue service.

Finally they had Neil breathing oxygen. He was incapable of dressing himself so they did that, too, and then dressed themselves and secured their climbing harnesses, put on their helmets, complete with head torches, and fastened their crampons. Only then did they step into the darkness of the night, onto the lethal ice.

'It's all downhill from here.' Billy tried to make a joke but Juliet gave a shiver.

'The one good thing about climbing in the dark is that you can't see the gradient,' she muttered as she clipped herself onto the fixed rope and felt her crampons bite hard into the ice.

Neil was sandwiched between Finn and Billy, virtually carried down by the combined efforts of the two men.

Juliet trudged slowly behind, forcing her drowsy, foggy brain awake. One mistake—just one mistake here—and she'd slide five thousand feet down the icy Lohtse face and into a bottomless crevasse. The thought was enough to hone her concentration.

Their flashlights lit the blue ice as they moved slowly downwards, one step and then another. They paused to change Neil's oxygen bottle and have a drink and then finally, what seemed like hours later, they saw lights ahead of them and two Sherpas came to help them.

They had reached Camp II.

* * *

'It isn't low enough.' Lying in the tent, Finn looked drawn and tired. 'We need to get him lower. If we can take him down to Camp I tonight, he stands a chance of recovery.'

Juliet coughed and withdrew another injection of dexamethasone, which she pushed into Neil's thigh, straight through his down suit.

The injection seemed to revive him and he removed the oxygen mask and started talking.

'Thanks, guys.' He shook his head slightly. 'My head's feeling clearer.'

'Is it worth making him walk in a straight line?' Billy asked, but Juliet shook her head.

'You're right that we do the tandem gait test as a test for HACE, but it can persist for several days after descent so there isn't any point in doing that now. He was staggering and uncoordinated at Camp III so we're certain of our diagnosis.'

'Keep the oxygen on,' Finn instructed, as they all drank as much fluid as they could. He turned to Juliet. 'You could stay here.'

She knew that he was giving her the chance to rest but she also knew that Neil's medical condition was precarious and that if he deteriorated, Finn would need her help.

'I'm fine. I can make it to Camp I.' She was actually feeling stronger and wondered whether it was just the effect of being at a lower altitude. They were still high, of course, but there was proportionally more oxygen in the atmosphere than there had been up at Camp III.

They continued down the slope and arrived at Camp I as dawn was breaking.

By now Neil was walking under his own steam and had made a significant recovery.

'It's amazing what descent can achieve,' Finn muttered as he dropped into a tent next to Juliet. 'Well done, you. You're amazing.'

She was too exhausted to react to the praise. She just wanted to lie down, close her eyes and never open them again. But she knew that first she had to drink something or she ran the risk of becoming severely dehydrated, and that in turn would increase her susceptibility to altitude sickness. Having had such a close call with Neil, she had no intention of being the next victim.

So she forced herself to sit up and drink the tea handed to her by a smiling Sherpa and then she closed her eyes and allowed herself to relax. They were going to rest for a few hours and then tackle the dreaded icefall.

They spent the night at Camp I and then started out in darkness to tackle the icefall before the sun rose.

As Juliet fastened her crampons she reflected on the fact that she would only have to risk her neck on this section of the mountain a few more times.

Whether they decided to drop down into the valley for a few days or not, soon they'd be making the final push towards the summit.

She glanced over her shoulder for a moment, staring upwards at the harsh, unforgiving flanks of the world's highest mountain.

'Are you all right?' Finn was by her side, his gaze searching. 'You're thinking of Dan.'

She opened her mouth to deny it and then sighed. He knew her so well, there was no point in lying. 'I've never actually seen it before,' she confessed. 'Cerebral oedema. Not like that.' She glanced towards Neil who was fastening his crampons, his fingers remarkably steady. 'I keep wondering if that's what happened to Dan. I was so exhausted up there that if you and Billy hadn't been there to help, I never would have been able to muster the energy to do anything.'

'We all do what we can,' Finn said roughly, 'and up here, that's the best you can expect. You don't climb Everest expecting to be rescued if you get into trouble. You climb it, fully aware of the risks. Dan was aware of those risks, Jules.'

She nodded but felt the tears clog her throat. 'If you'd been with him—'

'The weather was bad and they think that the levels of oxygen in the air were even lower than usual,' Finn said quietly. 'If I'd been there, the chances are I would have died, too.'

She shook her head. 'You would have saved him, I know you would.'

He gave a wry smile and brushed her cheek with a gloved hand. 'I'm not God, Jules.'

Her breath caught as she stared up into his handsome face. At eight years old she'd thought Finn was a god. He'd been tall, strong and calm. In all the years she'd known him, she'd never seen him panic. He had been the perfect foil to her brother's wild nature. *And she couldn't ever have imagined a man more perfect than Finn.*

She frowned slightly, confused by her thoughts.

Finn watched her for a moment and then let his hand drop to his side. 'You're tired,' he said roughly. 'Let's get down.'

And he turned and trudged back to the tents to check on Neil, leaving Juliet to follow.

'I'm doing fine.' He smiled up at them both. 'No reason at all why I can't have a go at the summit in a few days' time.'

Juliet stared at him. 'Neil, for goodness' sake.'

He stood up and tested his crampons. 'I know I had a problem but it's gone now. You know as well as I do that people can develop altitude sickness and still go on to climb the mountain. I'm feeling great now. Really strong.' As if to prove his point, he heaved his pack onto his back and settled it in place.

Juliet was appalled. 'You're feeling fine because you're full of dexamethasone and bottled oxygen and because you're at a lower altitude,' she reminded him, unable to believe that he was even considering making an attempt on the summit. What was it about high mountains that tempted people into making reckless decisions? 'This isn't the place to play macho he-man, Neil,' she said gently. 'If you're not fit, you can't go up.'

The smile faded and Neil's expression was suddenly stubborn. 'Do you know how long I've waited for this moment? Do you know what this means to me?'

'Presumably not enough to risk death,' Juliet said quietly, and Neil glared at her.

'I know my own body.'

'You know as well as I do that climbers aren't always objective.' Juliet put a hand on his arm. 'You've been affected by altitude before, Neil. You know as well as I do that it's very likely to happen again.'

'People with HACE have gone on to the summit of Everest.'

'True,' Juliet agreed, 'but others have gone on to die. And that isn't going to happen to you. Not while I'm the doctor on this team.'

'Problem?' Billy crawled into their tent and Neil glared at him.

'She's saying that I can't make the summit this season.'

Billy rubbed a hand over his chin. 'You're too slow, Neil,' he said gruffly. 'There's no way you're going to make it to the top like that. You know it, and I know it.'

'I had HACE, that's why I was slow, but I'm OK now. A few days breathing the air of Base Camp and I'll be good as new. I can make it. I can get there.'

'And what about getting back?' Juliet's eyes flashed and pain burned inside her as she thought of her brother. 'Getting there is only half the trip, Neil. And more climbers die coming down the mountain because they use everything they've got to make the summit and they don't have anything left to get them back down.'

Neil's shoulders slumped. 'It's been my dream for so long…'

Finn put a hand on his shoulder. 'The mountain isn't going anywhere.' His voice was strong and steady. 'There are other years. Surviving as a climber is about making good decisions that are often difficult. Turning your back on the summit is probably the hardest decision any climber has to make.'

Neil breathed out heavily and all the fight seemed to drain out of him. Then he gave a nod. 'I know you're right—but it's hard…'

Impulsively Juliet put her arms round him and hugged him. 'Finn's right. There will be other years.'

She felt incredibly sad as they all finally moved out of Camp I on the final walk down to Base Camp. Everyone seemed preoccupied.

They plodded back down through the icefall, clipping themselves onto the lines and balancing across the ladders.

Finn was in the lead, followed by Neil and several other climbers. The Sherpas were behind them as they all worked their way back down to Base Camp.

The sun rose and Juliet stopped for a moment and sucked air into her starving lungs. No matter how hard she breathed, she still didn't feel that she was getting enough air.

Anyone who thought climbing Everest was easy had only ever done it from the comfort of their armchair at home, she thought wryly as she contemplated what lay ahead.

Even standing still, her body felt limp with fatigue and her lungs were bursting.

Ahead of her, Finn walked at a steady, even pace, looking as strong and comfortable as ever. He didn't seem to be struggling at all.

Juliet gave a resigned sigh, reminding herself that he'd always been good at high altitude. Some people were. And they were lucky. Some people just never managed to acclimatise. They were unlucky. She fell somewhere in between the two.

Unable to get herself moving again, she watched as Finn trudged forward across the snow. Suddenly the ice opened up beneath him and he dropped out of sight.

It was as if he'd been swallowed by the mountain.

For a moment Juliet just stared in horror, frozen to the spot and unable to move—unable to believe what had just happened.

And then suddenly she found her voice.

'Finn! Oh, God, Finn! No, no, no!' Her heart pounding and her hands sweaty with terror, she dropped to her knees and crawled forward, gasping for breath, staring down into the yawning, deep blue chasm of the crevasse.

Behind her she heard the shouts of other climbers and knew they'd seen what had happened and were moving forward to help.

She stared down, blinded by fear and panic. There was no bottom. It just went down and down…

And then she saw Finn lying on an ice shelf, his body immobile.

'Finn! Finn!' She was calling his name and sobbing now, great tearing sobs that made breathing even more difficult. She tugged at the rope, which was still attached to his climbing harness, as if her puny efforts would be enough to miraculously lift him from the edge of oblivion. 'Get up, get up! Please, wake up, get up. *Move!* Please, be all right, please. Oh, God, no, don't do this to me.'

He didn't stir and she felt hysteria rise inside her, a swirl of frantic, desperate emotion that she'd never encountered before.

For the first time in her life she knew real, mind-numbing fear.

He couldn't be dead. He couldn't. Not Finn.

'Juliet.' Billy was behind her, a firm hand on her shoulder, pulling her back from the edge. 'You have to move out of the way.'

'No!' She shrugged him off as tears flowed down her cheeks and she gave way to great gulping sobs. 'I won't leave him. I'm going down there. I'm a doctor. I can do something.' She scrabbled frantically at the rope and two Sherpas moved forward and gently pulled her away from the edge.

She struggled and fought but she was weakened by the lack of oxygen and the physical exertion of the past few days and she collapsed in a heap on the snow, overcome with grief.

'Juliet!' Billy frowned at her with a lack of comprehension. 'What the hell is the matter with you? What's the use of you throwing yourself down there after him? We need to work this out carefully or there'll be more than Finn in trouble. I've never seen you like this before. You never panic.'

Well, she was panicking now.

'We need to get him out.' One of the Sherpas was leaning over the edge and jerking on the rope. 'This isn't going to hold.'

Juliet closed her eyes, no longer able to look. They were going to retrieve Finn's body and she didn't want to be there to see it. And her own body seemed to have given up. Movement seemed pointless. She just wanted to sit on the icy slope and wait for the mountain to swallow her, too.

She felt empty and drained.

In the background she heard a series of shouts and dimly sensed a sudden flurry of activity but she still didn't move, her body shivering despite the increasing heat of the sun.

Endless time passed and she was dimly aware of people shouting instructions and lowering ropes. She knew she ought to be helping but she felt limp and lifeless and totally lacking in motivation. There was no way she could help them bring Finn's body out of that crevasse. It was too much to ask.

Her eyes blurred with tears and she glanced up, wondering what was taking them so long.

Then she saw Finn's ice axe come over the lip of the

crevasse, the top of his helmet appeared and then his broad shoulders as he pulled himself out.

Juliet stared, her emotions suspended, her breath trapped in her throat.

Finn lay for a moment on the snow, heaving in gulps of air, and then he struggled to his feet. 'Thanks, guys.' He gave a rueful smile and grimaced as he moved one shoulder gingerly, testing for damage. 'That was a close one.'

Billy slapped him on the back, relief evident in his face. 'You gave us all heart failure, man.'

'Just checking you were concentrating,' Finn drawled, his eyes drifting to Juliet who was still sitting in the snow, shaking. 'Jules? You look grim. What happened to you?'

Billy glanced between them, a sudden look of speculation on his face. 'I think you happened to her,' he said in a mild tone. 'You gave our good doctor the fright of her life. Maybe she was afraid you'd test her first-aid skills and she'd be left wanting.'

'Maybe.' Finn's gaze was fixed on Juliet, who still couldn't believe that he wasn't lying dead in the crevasse.

He was standing in front of her. Alive. And she just wanted to sob and sob with pure, undiluted relief.

'So…' Billy glanced towards the Sherpas, who were checking rope and using ice screws to secure a ladder, which was looking alarmingly precarious. 'Are you ready to go on down or do you want to rest here for a bit?'

Finn raised an eyebrow and glanced around him. 'Having dodged the jaws of death once here, I don't think it's a great idea to linger. Let's take our rest down at Base Camp. Juliet?'

She just looked at him, feeling too drained to move. 'I—I'm fine,' she croaked. 'Be there in a minute. You carry on.'

She needed a few moments to get herself together.

To recover from the shock of seeing Finn vanish into a crevasse.

She was so lost in her own thoughts that she didn't realise he'd crouched down beside her until she heard his rough male voice.

'Jules.' He spoke quietly, even though the other climbers and Sherpas were already moving out. 'Sweetheart, look at me.'

She was relieved she was wearing ice-goggles. At least they concealed the fact that she'd been crying.

She felt such a fool.

'I'm sorry I gave you a fright.' He slipped a gloved hand under her chin and lifted her face to his, his gaze suddenly speculative. 'Or maybe I'm not.'

'What are you talking about?'

'Well, it's certainly been interesting, watching your reaction. I thought you didn't care about me.'

She jerked her chin away from his hand and lumbered to her feet, no easy feat given the quantity of gear she was wearing. Her eyes flashed defensively. 'You fell into a crevasse, Finn! That's a pastime designed to give any girl a fright.'

'Right.' He stood up, too, his body unnervingly

close to hers. 'So you would have reacted that way if anyone had fallen in?'

She adjusted the pack on her back. 'Of course I would. So would you. No one wants accidents up here. We've had enough trauma with Neil. I just want to get down in one piece, along with everyone else.'

She wished he wouldn't stand so close. She had an almost uncontrollable urge to hurl herself into his arms and never move again.

It was just the shock, she told herself firmly as she straightened her rucksack.

He was silent for a moment and then nodded. 'I'm sure the Sherpas would be touched to know that you would have cried and sobbed if they'd had an accident.'

She gave a gasp of embarrassment and glanced over his shoulder, but the others had all moved away, leaving them alone. She gritted her teeth and felt the colour rise in her cheeks. 'I didn't sob.' He was making it sound like an unusual reaction. He was making it sound as though she—as if she…

Her face drained of colour as the truth finally hit her.

She loved him.

Oh, dear God, she loved him. Despite all her efforts and her promises to herself that she was never going to let it happen, she was crazily in love with Finn, and probably always had been.

He was right. He'd been right all along.

Panic shot through her.

'Jules?' He studied her face for a moment and then

turned to look at the view. 'I never thought I'd be pleased that I'd fallen down a crevasse.'

She struggled to find her voice, still in shock. 'You're pleased?'

'Oh, yes, I'm pleased. Because I finally know what I'm dealing with.' He turned back to face her, his voice suddenly soft. 'You love me, Jules.'

She froze. 'Well, I don't— I mean, I haven't exactly— You can't possibly…' Her voice tailed off, her heart pounding hard against her chest. Suddenly the air seemed thinner than usual, making breathing even more difficult.

Her thoughts were confused and tangled.

She didn't want to love him.

She didn't want to love anyone.

Finn watched her for a long moment and then glanced down the slope and raised his hand to Billy, indicating they were on their way. 'You love me, Jules. And before this trip is up, you're going to admit it.'

CHAPTER NINE

JULIET lay in her tent, drained and exhausted by the events of the past few days and all the emotions she'd experienced in the space of a few hours.

She'd watched Finn die in front of her, or so she'd thought, and for a brief, terrible moment she'd felt as though part of her had died with him.

The knowledge that she loved him so deeply terrified her.

She'd spent her life avoiding this situation.

She'd dated men, of course she had, but she'd never felt anything deeper than friendship for any of them. She'd made sure of it.

But now there was no avoiding her feelings. It had happened. And she had to decide what to do.

With a soft moan of frustration and confusion she sat up and raked her fingers through her tangled blonde hair.

A few hours earlier she'd managed to take a 'shower', thanks to some willing Sherpas and two buckets of water.

Base Camp was experiencing a brief warm spell and Juliet had risked stripping down to nothing behind a piece of plastic sheeting and covering herself in soap and shampoo. It had felt fantastic to scrub away the grime and dirt of the mountains.

She chewed her lip and reached for her portable stereo, trying to calm her tangled thoughts by listening to Mozart. It didn't work so she switched the CD player to heavy rock music. That didn't work either so she switched it off altogether and lay there, trying to make sense of her thoughts.

She didn't want to be in love with Finn.

Her gut clenched at the thought of what that could mean. He was a climber.

A climber, like her father and brother.

And that meant risk.

She needed time to think.

She needed to decide what she was going to do.

Neil was improving steadily but Finn had decided that it would be best for him to descend still further, to be on the safe side, and Juliet was to escort him down.

It meant spending a few days at lower altitude in the Sherpa villages before coming back up to Base Camp for the final climb through all four camps to the summit.

Finn shifted his pack onto his back and walked steadily through the tented village that was Base Camp before joining Neil and Juliet who were preparing to descend into the valley.

Juliet stared at him and he had the satisfaction of seeing her colour rise. 'What are you doing here?'

The day before, when they'd finally staggered into Base Camp, he'd left her on her own in her tent to sleep and recover, sensing that it would be a bad time to push her.

He was willing to give her space.

But not too much space.

With a wry smile he acknowledged to himself that dealing with Juliet was not unlike tackling Everest. You had to proceed with caution, watch for signs and be careful on the ice. And with Juliet he was very definitely walking on ice.

'I'm coming with you,' he said calmly, giving Neil a friendly nod and noting that the other man was looking a great deal better after his close call.

Her eyes widened. 'Why are you coming with us?'

Because you're in love with me and this time I'm not letting you escape, he thought. 'Because it's the best way of gathering your strength for the summit push,' he said casually. 'The forecast is looking good for the end of the week. All being well, our team will be up at Camp IV by Friday. Then we'll sit it out until we have a break in the weather.'

Neil gave a grunt. 'I can't say I envy you,' he said quietly. 'Frankly, all I want now is to go home.' He'd lost his energy and his spirit during his ordeal, but Finn had known that would return. 'Do you think I'll be able to give it a go another year, or will the same thing happen?'

Finn pulled a face. 'Hard to say. It's true that if you've suffered HACE once, it's more likely to happen again,' he said honestly, 'but people have gone on to summit so it's certainly possible. You just have to be aware that the risk is always there.'

The risk was there for all of them.

And Finn was more and more determined that Juliet wasn't going to make that final climb. He knew that she didn't have the physical strength that she'd need to keep her going to the top.

And he didn't intend to lose her.

They put Neil on a helicopter that would take him back to Kathmandu and then Finn took her to a little teahouse perched on the green slopes.

After weeks of staring at snow, ice and the stark, stony moraine of Base Camp, it was wonderful to see vegetation. It felt like being in another world.

They were given a room with two bunks and a fire that burned erratically in the corner.

Juliet dropped her pack in the middle of the room, sank onto the bunk and stared into the fire, her heart thumping madly in her chest.

For the first time since they'd set out on this expedition they were alone together. *Truly alone.* The knowledge sent shivers of wicked excitement through her body.

She didn't dare look at Finn but she was aware of his every movement—the flex of his shoulders as he removed his own pack, the intensity of his gaze as he studied her in silence. And she knew he was looking at her because she could feel it.

'Jules.' Finn was the one to break the throbbing silence. 'Are you going to look at me?'

She turned her head and looked.

The tension in the room snapped tight and she was relieved that she was sitting down because she suddenly felt her knees weaken and her legs shake.

'Finn…' His name was a whisper on her lips and then he crossed the room in two strides and hauled her roughly to her feet, before taking her face in his hands and lowering his mouth to hers.

His kiss was hot and hard and she gave a moan of relief. This was what she needed. *What she'd dreamed of.* Since that one kiss in the tent, she'd spent an inordinate amount of time thinking about kissing Finn.

When she hadn't been concentrating on where to place her feet on a treacherous slope or examining a patient for signs of altitude sickness, she'd often found herself thinking of kissing Finn.

No man kissed like Finn.

It was a relentless seduction, a steady slide into the mindless oblivion of sexual excitement. *An outlet for all the tension and pressure of the past few weeks.* And, just like climbing, for this brief moment in time life was reduced to the physical.

They kissed as though it might be the last time they touched, with a passion that bordered on the desperate.

She felt the hardness of his body against hers, the rough scrape of his stubble against her skin.

And then a clear vision of Everest came into her head and she remembered that in the next few days this man would be aiming for the summit.

Would he make it, or would he die like her father and her brother?

And if he made it this time, what about the next time? The next mountain…

She gave a gasp and dragged her mouth away from his. 'This is a mistake.'

'The mistake was letting you run.' He buried his face in her neck. 'And not dragging you back where you belong. With me. You're never running again, Jules.'

She felt the warm slide of his hands under her shirt and felt the images in her brain fade. Suddenly she found she couldn't hold on to a single coherent thought. Her head was spinning and for once it had nothing to do with altitude. She could no longer remember why this wasn't a good idea because suddenly it seemed like the best idea in the world. *The only thing she wanted.* 'Finn…'

'I need you naked. Now.' His hands strong and urgent, he stripped her clothes off and then ran a hand slowly over the curve of her hip with undisguised masculine appreciation. 'You're stunning.'

'I'm thin.'

'Beautiful.' He bent his head and kissed her again and flames of passion licked through her veins and set her body on fire.

Her hands tugged at the front of his shirt and she fumbled with the buttons, almost sobbing with relief when he lifted his hands to help her, his mouth still on hers.

When they were both naked, he lifted her and laid her in front of the fire, slowly combing his fingers through her hair as he studied her face.

It had been so long.

Too long.

'Touch me.' She was desperate now, her body writhing beneath the hard, male pressure of his. She ran her hands over his back, over smooth, hard muscle and sleek, heated skin and then gave a soft gasp as he slid his tongue over her breast to her nipple and sucked her into the warmth of his mouth.

Excitement exploded inside her, driving her skyward.

She made a last, frantic attempt to remember the reasons why she shouldn't be doing this but they slipped from her grasp and she arched her back and slid a thigh over his in blatant invitation.

She didn't care about yesterday or tomorrow.

She only cared about now.

Her senses were throbbing and tangled, her body screaming for satisfaction. She ached for him in every possible way. It was as if her very existence suddenly depended on this man.

And perhaps he understood the depth of her need or maybe he felt the same way because he covered her with his powerful body and thrust deep. She arched and cried out at the sheer perfection of it.

'Jules.' His voice was hoarse. 'Open your eyes.'

Had she closed them?

With a supreme effort she opened them and fell into the burning heat of his gaze. She wanted to look away but she couldn't. He held her trapped, his eyes locked with hers, his body deep in hers.

Possession.

It was the only word she could hold in her brain. She was his and he was hers.

'I love you.' He lowered his head and took her mouth but still his eyes held hers—watching, assessing. 'I love you.'

Nothing else existed.

Only this moment and this man.

She stared into his eyes, felt him deep inside her and the responding throb of her own body.

'And you love me, too.' His mouth brushed hers again, his tongue teasing and seductive. 'You know you do. Say it, Jules. *Say it.*'

'I love you.' The words that had been trapped inside her for so long spilled out and she breathed the words against his seeking mouth, 'I love you, Finn, I love you, I love you.'

She couldn't stop saying it, as if she were afraid she might never get the chance again. The words terrified her and she clung to him, as if holding him tight might keep him from harm.

He slid a hand under her hips and lifted her, moving deeper still so that personal boundaries no longer existed. They were one.

And all control snapped.

He took her and it felt good, so perfect and powerful that she gripped him tightly and urged him on, needing more, *needing it all.*

And when the explosion ripped through them both they clung together and let it take them over the edge, falling, tumbling, spinning into a place far beyond thought and reason.

They lay together, breathless, exhausted and shaken.

Finally Finn drew breath. 'So…' His male drawl held a hint of self-mockery. 'If I said that I'd missed you, would you believe me?'

Snuggled against him with her eyes closed, she smiled. 'Maybe.'

It was the gentle teasing of lovers. The sleepy exchange of words that followed intense physical release.

'I love you, Jules.'

The mood changed in an instant and she tensed in his arms. 'Finn—'

'Are you going to deny that you love me, too?' He rolled her under him, his weight pressing her into the mattress. 'Are you going to pretend that you said those words in the heat of passion?'

'No.' She shook her head, her heart thumping against her chest. 'I'm not going to deny it. It's true. I do love you.' She broke off, almost blind with terror at the depth of her feeling for him. 'But it isn't going to change anything. I can't help the fact that I love you, but I can control what I do about it.'

She knew that now.

It was the only way she could keep herself safe.

He inhaled sharply and she felt him tense. 'What do you mean by that?'

'I can't let you into my life, Finn,' she said hoarsely, 'no matter how much I love you. I just can't do it.'

'I'm already in your life.'

'That's true up to a point. But when we leave here we go our separate ways. I'm not having you in my life, Finn. I can't.'

He was silent for a long moment and when he finally spoke his voice was husky. 'Do you really think I'm willing to let you walk away from what we share a second time? I let you do it once before, Jules. I've regretted it ever since. I won't let you do it again.'

In the corner of the room the fire glowed, casting an eerie red light over the room.

She gazed up at him, saw the hard determination glinting in his dark eyes, and reached out a hand to touch his face.

'You have to let me go, Finn.' Tears clogged her throat. 'I'm begging you to let me go.'

'I can't do that.' He turned his head and kissed the palm of her hand. 'I'm not going to let you do this to us, Jules. Not again. Not this time. We're perfect together. And you know it.'

She did know it.

And that was why she couldn't share her life with him. The risks were too great.

She started to cry softly, the tears sliding down her cheeks. 'Don't ask me to do this, Finn, you can't ask me to do this.' The tears fell more swiftly and suddenly she was sobbing helplessly. 'Don't ask this of me. I can't lose another man I love to these mountains. I can't do it. My father died, my brother died. I can't do it again. Don't make me do it again.'

'I'm careful, sweetheart, I'm not going to die.'

'You can't say that! You don't know that!'

'I know that the only thing that ever really matters to me when I go up there is coming back,' he said quietly.

She'd heard him say that to other climbers, climbers so fired up by determination to reach the summit that they didn't think about the return journey until it was too late. *There would be other years. The mountain wasn't going anywhere.*

But then she thought of the crevasse…

'It doesn't matter how careful you are.' Her vision was blurred with tears. 'If you're up there then you're in danger.'

'There's danger everywhere, Jules,' he said quietly, 'only most of us live our lives pretending it isn't out there. We delude ourselves that we're in control but we've both seen enough in our medical careers to know that life is a lottery. At least when I'm climbing mountains I'm focused on the danger. And the most important thing is that I'm doing something I love. I don't want to spend my life trapped in a hospital working fourteen-hour days until I retire, and then find that life has passed me by. I want to live it now, my way, just as you do.'

It was all true, but she'd had a split second glimpse of her life without him when he'd dropped into the crevasse and the image had left her paralysed with fear. The same overwhelming fear she'd felt when she'd lost her father and then her brother.

Juliet thumped him with her fists, too exhausted to do any real damage. 'I hate you, actually,' she sobbed. 'I hate you, Finn, for making me feel this way, for making me vulnerable when I've spent my whole life avoiding this situation. I was OK until we came here. I was doing OK.'

'You were only half-alive,' Finn said softly, gripping her wrists and lifting her arms above her head. 'And that isn't the way for either you or I to live. Life doesn't come with guarantees, Jules, but when you have the chance of happiness you have to grab it with both hands.'

She couldn't stop crying and he gave a low curse.

'Don't cry.' Finn brushed away her tears with the pad of his thumb. 'Please don't cry. You have to stop now. I can't see you like this. Oh, hell, Jules, *stop it.*' He rolled onto his back and gathered her against him, holding her tight and safe until eventually she had no tears left and she lay limply against him. Then he stroked her damp hair away from her face with a gentle hand and kissed her softly, a wry smile on his handsome face. 'I've never had a woman howl in my bed before. Clearly my technique needs work.'

His attempt at humour finally helped her find the control she needed and she gave a sniff and scrubbed at her face with the back of her hand, embarrassed and exhausted by her outburst of emotion. 'I do hate you,' she murmured in sorrowful tones. 'I hate you for making me feel this way.'

'You don't hate me.' He kissed her gently and she shook her head.

'Part of me does.'

He was silent for a long moment. 'Do you want me to give up climbing?'

She sighed. 'You couldn't. Any more than I could. It's part of who you are and why I love you. I wouldn't ask you to do it.'

'Then you just have to accept that I'll be coming home to you.'

She shook her head, still struggling with the fear inside her. 'Finn, I can't.'

He covered her mouth with his fingers. 'Don't say anything else. Not now. But when I'm safely down from Everest, you're going to have me in your life.'

She stared up at him, wanting to argue but too emotionally exhausted to speak, and she realised that none of it mattered any more. Tomorrow didn't matter.

All that mattered was now.

And she slid her arms round his neck and lifted her face for his kiss.

CHAPTER TEN

Camp IV, 7,900 metres above sea level

THE wind on the South Col howled and battered the tiny tents as if questioning their right to be this high on the mountain.

Breathing in oxygen from the small cylinder Juliet wondered yet again what on earth she was doing there.

They were in position, waiting for a break in the weather, a drop in the lethal winds that would mean that they could make their final assault on the summit. Fifteen hours of climbing without food or drink because this high up, removing a glove could mean losing a hand.

She was trying to drink in preparation but couldn't keep anything down.

If her few, blissful days down in the valley had done anything to bolster her flagging reserves of energy, she'd forgotten it now.

'Jules?' Billy lumbered into the tent with Finn. 'We need to talk to you.'

Talk? She looked at them blankly, wondering what gave them the impression that she had the energy to talk. Her brain wasn't working. Her mouth wasn't working. She wasn't sure that any of her body was working. She was cold. She was tired. And she felt as though she'd emptied her reserves.

They obviously thought so, too.

'You need to go down.' It was Finn who spoke, his tone blunt and clear so that there could be no mistake. 'You were slow on the climb from Camp III. You're never going to make it up to the summit and back.'

For a moment she just stared at him, her brain working in slow motion. And then she shook her head. 'I can do it.'

Finn swore under his breath and he gripped her arms, his fingers biting into her flesh. 'You were the one who told Neil to go down and you probably saved his life. I'm going to say the same thing to you that we said to him. This mountain isn't going anywhere. There will be other years.'

She shook her head. 'Not for me—this is my year. I'm almost there.'

Finn exhaled sharply. 'Do you realise what still lies between you and the summit? Fifteen hours of heavy slog, that's what. And just when you think you can't go any further you reach the Hilary Step and you have to climb up an ice face that requires energy that you're just not going to have. And if you do make it to the summit, what then, Jules?' His voice was harsh and he was still gripping her arms tightly. 'How are you planning to get down? Fly?'

Why did he sound so angry? She licked dry lips. The doctor in her knew that she was already dehydrated but at this altitude they just couldn't melt enough snow for their needs. It took too long.

Finn touched her arm. 'Go down, Juliet,' he urged. 'I'll come back with you. Or Mingma, the Sherpa from the Australian expedition, will go with you. Wait for us at Camp II. That way you'll be in a position to help if anything goes wrong for us.'

She stirred. The altitude had dulled the workings of her brain. She should be feeling sick disappointment as her dream slid through her fingers. And then she re- alised that the reason she didn't feel disappointed was nothing to do with the altitude.

Something opened inside her, something she'd kept locked down for years, and suddenly she understood. She understood everything. She understood that the reason she didn't feel disappointed was because this wasn't her dream.

Finn was right. It had been her brother's dream.

And suddenly she knew that she wasn't going to make the mistakes he had.

She lifted her head, removed her oxygen mask and gave Finn a weak smile. 'I'm going down. Finn, you go up. Do it for me.'

Juliet huddled in a tent at Camp II, drinking and try- ing to regain some of the energy she'd need to get down from the mountain.

But all she could think about was Finn.

He was up there, high on the mountain, one of the most exposed and dangerous places on earth.

Anxiety gnawed at her as she listened to the wind.

It was going to happen again.

Yet again she was going to lose someone she loved in these mountains. She was going to have to—

'Dr Adams.' A climber from another expedition put a radio in her hand, a broad grin on his face. 'There's a call for you.'

She'd been so deep in thought, so consumed by her own terror and imagination, that it took her a moment to realise that he'd just handed her a radio. Finally she spoke, her heart thudding. 'This is Dr Adams speaking.'

'Hi, sweetheart.'

'Finn?'

'I'm on the summit. I've made it.' His voice was so clear he could have been in the tent next door. It was impossible to believe he was on the roof of the world. 'I bet you're worrying so I wanted to tell you that I'm fine. The wind has dropped, we're on the top and it's beautiful up here.'

Something lifted and cleared inside her.

She couldn't believe he sounded so normal. After such a phenomenal athletic achievement he should be exhausted. She assumed it must be the adrenaline kicking in.

She smiled at the radio, tears of relief filling her eyes. 'I'm so pleased for you, Finn.' And she was. Really pleased. She knew how many times he'd been thwarted in his attempts to climb Everest. How many times he'd sacrificed his own ambitions for his own safety or to help another climber. 'It's your dream.'

'Not my whole dream.'

There was a pause and she was aware of an air of expectation in the tent—of other climbers looking at her curiously.

'Finn?'

The radio crackled. 'This has been a hard slog, but loving you is even harder. Tell me that you'll have me in your life, Jules. Tell me that you'll marry me when I get down from here.'

He was on top of Everest. *And he was proposing?*

She knew that everyone at Base Camp would be listening in, as well as the climbers at the other camps.

'Finn.' Her throat tightened. 'You know I can't.'

'Yes, you can. You can. You're going to say that you don't want me in your life. But what sort of a life is that going to be, Jules? Have you seriously thought about that?'

She already knew the answer to that.

Empty.

The radio crackled again. 'You're settling for less than you can have, and you've never been a woman to do things by halves. It just isn't you.'

She closed her eyes. 'Finn—'

'Some people go through their whole lives never knowing what it is to truly love. I'm not letting you throw what we have away. It's time to stop running, Jules. Time to use some of that courage in a different way. When I walk into Base Camp, you're going to marry me.'

One of the other climbers checked his watch. 'They need to get off that summit,' he muttered. 'They've been up there too long already.'

Juliet felt her heart flip. 'Finn.' Her voice was urgent as she spoke into the radio. 'You have to come down. You have to come down *now!*'

'Not until you've answered my question.' She could have sworn he was laughing but she decided she must have imagined it.

'Finn—'

'Just say yes, Jules. It's just you and me, sweetheart.'

And half the world listening in.

She took a deep breath. 'Yes. Yes!' Her voice cracked and she felt the colour rush into her cheeks. 'Now, come down so that I can kill you.'

He laughed and cut the connection.

Base Camp was in party mood.

The first climbers of the season had reached the summit and returned to Camp IV without mishap. So far all was well.

Juliet busied herself in the clinic, seeing an endless round of patients with minor ailments caused from staying too long at altitude. All of them winked, slapped her on the shoulder and congratulated her.

Thanks to Finn's surprise proposal from the summit, everyone knew about their relationship.

She should have felt light—happy—but she couldn't relax, couldn't concentrate properly on anything, until he was safely down.

There was always a risk of avalanche and he still had the treacherous icefall to negotiate. Overwhelmed by fear, she sank onto the nearest crate and put her head in her hands.

'Worrying again. You've got to learn to trust me, Jules.' Finn's voice came from the doorway of the tent, deep and male and the best thing she'd ever heard in her life.

Her eyes flew open with relief and joy. 'You're alive.'

'What sort of a greeting is that? Of course I'm alive.' He strolled into the tent and stood in front of her, his handsome face drawn and tired but his eyes bright with a fire that she couldn't ever remember seeing before.

She stood up, suddenly feeling ridiculously shy and elated at the same time. 'You came back…'

'I came back to you. And I'm going to carry on coming back to you, Jules.' He cupped her face and kissed her fiercely before dragging his mouth away from hers with a reluctant groan. 'Do you really think I'd ever jeopardise this? The most important thing in my life?' He dragged her into his arms, holding her so tightly she could hardly breathe.

She closed her eyes and felt his strength wrap itself around her. And then she remembered just what he'd achieved. 'I'm so proud of you.' She pulled away and smiled up at him. 'You did it. Your dream. Dan's dream.'

He stared down at her in silence, studying every angle of her face. 'My dream is here,' he said softly, stroking her hair away from her cheeks, 'with you. And always will be.'

Her stomach tumbled and colour filled her cheeks. 'I can't believe you proposed to me from the summit of Everest. Everyone was listening.'

He smiled. 'I wanted to do it in public to make it harder for you to say no. And I wanted it to be memorable. Something we can tell our children.'

She stilled. 'Children?'

'Yes, children. And don't tell me that people like us shouldn't have children.' His expression grew serious. 'Jules, our children are going to be the luckiest children in the world. They're going to have exciting, unpredictable lives with parents who adore them.'

She chewed her lip. 'But what if—?'

'"What if" is no way to live a life,' he said softly. '"What if" stops you reaching for your dreams and fulfilling them. You can't live your life in fear that something might go wrong.' His eyes were suddenly gentle. 'You've lost two people who were very close to you and you want to find some way of making sure it doesn't happen again to you or anyone else you love. But you can't do it, angel. Life is sometimes bad and sometimes good and we owe it to ourselves to enjoy the good when it comes our way. The bad might never happen and if it does, we'll deal with it.'

She took a deep breath, needing to talk about how she'd felt. 'I was devastated when I lost the baby. When

I discovered I was pregnant I waited to feel shocked and horrified, but I never did. Losing it was terrible.'

'And we didn't even really talk about it.'

She shook her head, knowing that the responsibility for that lay with her. 'I just couldn't.'

'I gave you too much space. I should have forced you to talk. Been more honest about my own feelings,' he confessed. 'But I was afraid I'd frighten you off. I'd always loved you, Jules.'

'I thought you were marrying me because of the baby.'

He pulled a face. 'I got my timing wrong. I should have proposed before the baby but I knew how scared you were of commitment and marriage so I was trying to find the right way. And before I could find the right way, you fell pregnant. And after that there was no way I could convince you I was marrying you because I loved you. I decided that I'd just have to show you over time. But you ran out on me and then your brother died—and after that there was too much between us.'

'We've wasted so much time.'

'No.' He shook his head, his arms still locked around her. 'If we could have made it work ten years ago, we probably would have done it. Circumstances were against us. But we've been given another chance. I want you to marry me. And before you answer, you ought to know that I don't need you to stay in one place,' he said roughly. 'I know you need variety and space and you can have that within our marriage. I have a house in the Lake District with roses round the door and three acres of land backing onto the fells. My friends are climbers. When I'm not climbing or on the lecture circuit, I work in an A and E unit where lots of the staff are in the local mountain rescue team. We can live there for as much of the year as you like or, if you don't like that idea, we can travel, climb or whatever makes you happy.'

He was offering her the world on a plate.

'You make me happy.' She smiled up at him, tears in her eyes. 'It's being with you that makes me happy.'

She knew that now. A life without him would be sterile and cold. A life half lived.

His eyes searched hers. 'Does that mean you're saying yes?'

'I'm saying yes.' And she reached up and kissed him.

0306/03a

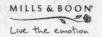

MILLS & BOON® 0306/03b

Live the emotion

_MedicaL
romance™

HER BOSS AND PROTECTOR by Joanna Neil

Dr Jade Holbrook's first day in A&E doesn't go as planned. She discovers her landlord, Callum Beresford, is also her new boss! Jade knows she hasn't made a good impression on the handsome consultant, and is aware that he is watching her every move…

A&E DRAMA: Pulses are racing in these fast-paced dramatic stories

THE SURGEON'S CONVENIENT FIANCÉE
by Rebecca Lang

Theatre Nurse Deirdre Warwick is determined that the two children left in her care will have the best life possible. When Dr Shay Melburne enters her life suddenly, Deirdre finds herself falling hopelessly in love with him – and then he offers her a marriage of convenience…but can he offer her his love?

THE SURGEON'S MARRIAGE RESCUE
by Leah Martyn

Adam Westerman is a successful Sydney surgeon and has returned to the Outback to find the beautiful ex-wife he's never managed to forget. Charge nurse Liv Westerman fears Adam has only come for custody of their child. She finds herself hoping that he has come back for both of them…!

On sale 7th April 2006

Available at WHSmith, Tesco, ASDA, Borders, Eason, Sainsbury's and most bookshops

www.millsandboon.co.uk

FREE!

4 Books
and a surprise gift!

We would like to take this opportunity to thank you for reading this Mills & Boon® book by offering you the chance to take FOUR more specially selected titles from the Medical Romance™ series absolutely FREE! We're also making this offer to introduce you to the benefits of the Reader Service™—

- ★ **FREE home delivery**
- ★ **FREE gifts and competitions**
- ★ **FREE monthly Newsletter**
- ★ **Exclusive Reader Service offers**
- ★ **Books available before they're in the shops**

Accepting these FREE books and gift places you under no obligation to buy, you may cancel at any time, even after receiving your free shipment. Simply complete your details below and return the entire page to the address below. You don't even need a stamp!

YES! Please send me 4 free Medical Romance books and a surprise gift. I understand that unless you hear from me, I will receive 6 superb new titles every month for just £2.80 each, postage and packing free. I am under no obligation to purchase any books and may cancel my subscription at any time. The free books and gift will be mine to keep in any case.

M6ZEF

Ms/Mrs/Miss/Mr ....Initials..
BLOCK CAPITALS PLEASE

Surname ....

Address...

....

....Postcode ....

Send this whole page to:
UK: FREEPOST CN81, Croydon, CR9 3WZ